BLOOD OF THE WOLF

About the Author

Charles Mackie is the pseudonym adopted by Dr JCM MacDonald before he retired from Medical practice in Elgin. He is the author of the Wolf Trilogy, researched and written in the lulls during busy days and nights as a general practitoner and anaesthetist, hugely encouraged by Irene his wife and by his children.

His interest in Alexander Stewart, better known as The Wolf of Badenoch, has been life long, nurtured by a love for and intimate knowledge of the soft, colourful land and exciting history of the Laich of Moray but stimulated by Lochindorb, the awesome lair of The Wolf. Throughout all three novels a curiosity to learn about the bond between Alexander Stewart, Kings son, and Mariota de Athyn, femme fatale and mother to his vivid family has guided Charles Mackie's thoughts, his imagination and his pen.

Also written by the author

The Wolf

First Published	1977	Robert Hale	ISBN 0 7091-5777-0
Second Edition	2001	Gopher Publishing	ISBN 90-76953-20-1
Third Edition	2003	Librario Publishing	ISBN 1-90440-18-5

Mariota

First Published	1981	Robert Hale	ISBN 0-7091-8877-3
Second Edition	2003	Librario Publishing	ISBN 1-90440-33-9

Blood of The Wolf

First Published	1978	Robert Hale	ISBN 0-7091-6965-5
Second Edition	2006	Librario Publishing	ISBN 1-90440-75-4

ISBN: 1-904440-75-4

Copies can be ordered via the Internet
www.librario.com

or from:

Brough House, Milton Brodie, Kinloss
Moray IV36 2UA
Tel/Fax No 00 44 (0)1343 850 617

Printed and bound by
DigiSource (GB) Ltd, Livingston

Blood of the Wolf

by

Charles Mackie

Librario

Introduction

An earlier book has described how a treasure of Scottish mediaeval literature came to be unearthed in a dungeon of the Palace of the Bishops at Spynie in Moray. This discovery, six hundred years after the nearby Elgin Cathedral was burnt by the Wolf of Badenoch, was a remarkable stroke of luck, for the Winchester Papers, the contents of a Bishop's reliquary, revealed contemporary knowledge of people and deeds that increase or modify our understanding of mediaeval Scotland and in particular of Alexander Stewart, prince of the realm, the Wolf of Badenoch. Bishop John Winchester, in precise square script, committed to parchment his conclusions about events that led up to the burning of the Cathedral of Elgin and his opinion of the two protagonists. These conclusions were contrary to the established legend and they must have come dangerously close to heresy. There were other matters too, concealed in that leaden chest which, in 1450, would have hung him for treason. He ruled the Bishopric of Moray in days when men trod a cautious tightrope between the rule of law and the rule of might. These were the dark years of our history when murder struck in fortress and in field and the shadow of the Black Douglas chilled the Kingdom of Scotland. John Winchester remained a favourite of King James II because he buried his opinions under a hundredweight slab of Caithness slate.

For me, the discovery of these documents provided the fascinating autobiography of Sir Philip Hogeston, Knight of Duffus, already published as *The Wolf*. Two years after I had written that tale and had returned, I thought, to my mundane twentieth-century affairs for ever, a telephone call from my friend John Hamilton so unsettled me that I had no choice but to plunge metaphorically once more into the mysterious and muddied waters of the great loch of Spynie that lapped the home and ordered the lives of Philip and Bridget Hogeston.

"Is that you Mac?" Hamilton, curator of the museum of Antiquities which held, on loan, the Winchester Papers, is as solid as Schiehallion and usually unexcitable but over the telephone that evening his voice raised the hairs on the back of my neck.

"I have something for you, something that is going to shake your confidence in Sir Philip Hogeston's story and get you going all over again." There was a long pause through which his breathing from one hundred and forty miles away built up my adrenalin like the ticking of a time-bomb.

"Can you remember the Bishop's Riddle? I think I have an answer to part of it."

That was enough and I was off next morning on the road to Dalwhinnie and central Scotland.

I left early and stopped as I came level with Lochindorb. I can never pass the gap in the hills without reliving the excitement of that period in Philip Hogeston's life which took him into the haunt of the Wolf. Dense dawn mist clung to the loch and on this pearl grey carpet the castle floated like a golden antique framed by pastel greens of the hills beyond. It was an unearthly sight.

I was alone in the mountains of Badenoch with the ghosts of the people of Lochindorb Castle, Murdo and Hilda, James and Duncan, Philip and Big Walt, and the Wolf and Mariota, and I recalled the Bishop's conundrum:

"Mariota the baud or Lady Jean Hay
Truth and Time will ever gainsay
Wha slew the Wolf and his Whelp of Garth –
Adultery witchcraft or God's Own Wrath."

This book is the result of an attempt by John Hamilton and myself to read that riddle. Because of it the story has three beginnings and some may think like I do, as yet no end.

One

Beyond Dalmally, myrtle and birch bowed to stunted pines and juniper as the forest marched south. Rain pulled its skirts over loch and islands and like a bad hem the track ahead dipped between treeline and mountain before vanishing into the Pass of Brander. June 1439 had been wet beyond the recall of old men and the steeps of Cruachan wept torrents that roared in rainbow cloud into Loch Awe.

A knot of horsemen came out of the birch wood, their steel casques and breastplates flashing in a passing finger of sunlight. They halted. The leader rode carefully from cover and urged his horse down a peaty channel to a gash in the hillside. He was a tall lean man in black armour. He steadied his mount and peered through the fine drizzle at the slope of Ben Cruachan.

"John Gorm." A man on a piebald stallion joined him. He was younger than his leader but as formidable. His gloved hand caressed his horse's cheek, his long arms sprouting from a leather jerkin, his head encased in a helmet hung with chain mail. The older man pointed.

"The blockhouse is there." James Stewart's iron clad arm indicated a low square stone building just visible against the grey wet rock of the mountain.

"To pass it is to part with secrecy: I shall ambush them here. Hogeston is hard on our tail and we shall not have long to wait. I would have wished to kill him in the lands of Lorn but it will suffice if the news reaches Stirling that a Queen's messenger was ambushed and slaughtered by a black knight."

Behind them a curlew called and the two men turned instantly towards the sound. High on the moor a man waved and pointed his left arm to Dalmally. His right hand was held steadily above his head.

9

"A single rider is coming through the wood," said John Gorm Stewart to his father.

"I have eyes." James Stewart pulled off a glove, put a finger to his lower lip and gave three trilling calls in reply. The knot of horsemen under the birch trees broke and vanished.

Minutes passed before the rider came into view, stopped when he saw two armed men, hesitated, then spurred his horse towards them.

"If you are one of Sir Philip Hogeston's men why are you alone and where is your master?"

The black knight spoke quietly and without menace.

"I am John Sime, smith of Duffus," replied the man. "I am riding ahead of Sir Philip to Dunstaffnage with letters for the Queen and the Black Knight of Lorn."

"I am a black knight as you can see," said Stewart. "Give me the letters." Sime dismounted and drew a package from his saddlebag. Behind him men approached quietly.

"Seize him," commanded Stewart.

"For God's sake sir," cried the smith. "I come in peace. These letters are for you and Queen Joan."

"Strip him," said Stewart and, half naked, Sime was bound to the trunk of a silver birch.

"Now use him as target practice." The knight on the black horse swung his steed as if to go.

"Mercy Sir, for the love of Christ," yelled Sime. "I have done you no harm." Forty paces away eight men reached for their quivers. "If murder me you must, first tell me why," screamed the man from Duffus.

The black knight looked at him. His eyes laughed at his victim. "The mistake you made, your fatal mistake, was to assume that I am the Black Knight of Lorn, master of Dunstaffnage, protector and new wed husband of the Queen," said Stewart.

"Dead, killed as if by brigands for your gear, you will be of use to me. With these papers I shall enter the land of Lorn and once there –" he paused. His eyes were fixed on some other thing and blackened teeth showed in a grim smile. "Once there," he repeated, "I will slocken my hate with the blood of Philip Hogeston." He spat out the words, turned, and eight arrows ripped into John Sime the smith of Duffus.

Two

Bridget Hogeston stood at the door of Plewlands and watched her men ride into the oak wood. Rain clouds rolled away over the Moray Firth and the sun blazed from a blue sky. She could hear the troop of horse faintly in the forest, out of sight now, hidden by a steamy mist that rose from the lawn and the sodden flowerbeds. She lifted her gown above her ankles and took off her shoes. She had not felt the soft dampness of summer earth since she was a girl and as she walked over the grass the feel of the warm moist turf on her bare feet reminded her of Normandy and of Philip. In the autumn when they met they had walked one morning under the elms and beeches to her favourite bower by the brook that chuckled its way towards Evreux and the river Seine. She had slipped off her shoes but before she could wade the stream Philip whisked her into his arms, carried her across and dropped her on wet earth amongst the buttercups. Warm sticky mud oozed between her toes and she screamed at him. Then, pulling up her skirts, she fled along the river bank revelling in the new sensation. Philip had laughed and called pretty things after her flying legs. He had wanted to make love to her but although she had teased him terribly the ecstasy remained for her wedding night.

There was the day of the tournament at her father's castle of Dreux, a very special day for her. She remembered a low October sun slanting across wooded hills, softening the reds, greens and azure blues on tabards and horse-cloaks and burnishing dull armour to silver and gold. For the first time in years she thought now of the black beard and sharp eyes of André de Pacy, her other suitor and the dismay and anger which had sped in turn across her father's face when his champion fell to her

Scotsman's lance. Philip had dismounted, his hair loose on the evening breeze and in atrocious French with a growl of Scottish rrrs he claimed his reward as "Victorr Ludorrum." She had barely managed to control her giggles as she waited for her Father's reply.

"Very well, my brave Scottish friend, get to your feet and name your prize." And in a voice that everyone could hear, Philip had said, "I ask for the hand of Lady Bridget."

Oh the joy and pride she had felt and the dreadful fear lest her father should refuse.

She stood beside the rose beds in Plewlands garden and placed a bare foot on freshly turned earth. Had that been so long ago? She sighed. Long enough to lose two sons in battle and to suffer a hundred partings from Philip. She plucked the rain spoilt blooms and saw ants already working among fallen petals and ladybirds waiting for the greenfly. A blackbird hopped across the lawn, head cocked for the sound of a dew worm. Mark the gardener came into the orchard and Bridget slipped on her shoes.

"Bonjour madame!" the gardener said and touched his forehead. She liked the way he copied the rich Provencal accent of his father. Mark was as Scottish as an oatcake but in her company he mixed his broad Moray vowels with the most unlikely French idiom. She talked to him, anxious to take her mind off the tall leather back of her husband who had ridden out from Plewlands and, it might be, from her life. She led him round the orchard, admired the well-formed apple crop, the cluster of plums and the ripening cherries and left him at the hives, afraid of the venomous little creatures although she admired the skilful way Mark worked his smoke amongst them before stealing their honey. His father, Jules, had had the same knack and made a ready groat peddling his bee-sting cures for rheumatics.

Jules had been her favourite amongst the serfs, the handsome bull that he was, and had shared a secret with her which she had kept for a long time even from her husband. Two years after she came to Scotland Philip had to leave her. The English were invading and the Earl rallied his men of Moray to ride against them. When they had gone, Bridget arranged to be invited to his castle at Avoch on the Black Isle as the guest of the wife of the guardian. There was a pressing need for Bridget to travel north. The purple shadow of Mariota de Athyn, mistress of the Wolf of Badenoch had fallen between herself and Philip. Until that time, she had been sure of her man. His past life was full of adventure, at the Crusade, and before as Prisoner of the Wolf in Lochindorb castle. Her inquisitive French mind had made him speak, freely she thought, of the wild Stewarts of Badenoch, and of his captor, and of Mariota. But in Duffus, lived a woman, Phoebe Corbett, a fortune-teller, a "speywife," with a wicked tongue. Bridget hated her and had torn into this Jezebel for uttering malicious gossip about one of her servants, Lizzy, and the blacksmith's son. A week later the same little Lizzy came to her in hysterics with a tale she had been told by Phoebe about the master. From her sobs Bridget pieced together the information that the Duffus speywife had warned Lizzy to "look out for the master when he is on his own, for why had he to flee the country when he was a young pup if not for fornicating with the Wolf's mistress?" Bridget was furious. With half her mind she told herself that what her husband had done before they met was his own business. The other half, the jealous half, cried out that public gossip about her Philip was very much her affair. She rode to Phoebe Corbett's home and warned her that if she spread such lies she would have her denounced as a witch. The threat was enough and it was many years before she heard that slanderous tale again. But it had unsettled her and there and then she determined to meet Mariota Athyn.

Bridget knew that the Wolf's mistress had moved from the castle in Mar to which she had been banished by her husband and was living at Dornoch with her daughter Margaret, Countess of Sutherland. Dornoch, she thought was not far from Avoch and so, escorted by a small detachment of the castle garrison, she travelled to the Black Isle. They sailed up the Moray Firth from Findhorn and Bridget spent two weeks with Hermione Chisholm, wife of the guardian. When she was leaving, she told her hostess that she planned to travel home through Inverness to show off her retinue, but at the Muir of Ord she ordered the soldiers to wait and with only Lizzy and Jules for company rode north to Dornoch. Everything so far had been carefully planned with one intention, to meet and talk with the woman Mariota. The journey was long and tiring. She hadn't imagined Scotland to be such a desert of mountain, forest and wretched squalid homes. In Embo she spent a night at an inn which, joy of joys, provided her with a tub and hot water to scrub off the Highland dirt. Jules rode ahead with her letter to Mariota Athyn and returned with an invitation written and sealed by the Earl of Sutherland asking her to stay at his castle for as long as she wished. There was also a note of hand from the Athyn woman.

"It will pleasure me greatly to see you, mistress Bridget Hogeston, and to talk with you about all things to your interest concerning my family the Stewards of Lochindorb. The regard in which I hold your husband Philip is matched only by my desire to greet you and I am flattered that you should have journeyed so far to meet

Your Friend Mariota."

Bridget studied the letter. The handwriting was plainly set down by a scribe but the tone, she thought, held a hint of patronage, or was it levity? She wondered if she had said too much in her message but she was sure that her request to meet and talk with Mariota had been non-committal. The swiftness of the response and the direct reference to Philip unnerved her. It had taken Mariota less time to fathom her purpose than it had taken her to write the letter.

She stayed in the castle for a week and left laden with gifts. Mariota was kind and disarming and her daughter Margaret an obliging hostess, yet as she rode from Dornoch, Bridget asked herself if that beautiful tragic woman was real or if the part had been played by an actress of consummate skill. During her stay her mind had been filled with the picture of this sad creature full of life and love but denied the affections of her husband, a bold and proud man, maimed and made impotent by the oldest and most terrible of the world's diseases. It was a horrifying tale but as she rode from that land of mist and mountain she felt as if she had sojourned in a dream-world. Facts slipped from her. Had the dread word leprosy been used or in the course of her stay with that extraordinary woman had she been skilfully led to imagine a situation which blinded her with horror and pity? She had arrived home more confused, more unsettled, and more jealously in love with Philip than ever before.

Bridget brought herself back to the present. She left Mark and his bees and walked to the edge of the forest which surrounded her gardens and her orchards. Plewlands glowed against the greens of oak, beech and yew, sunlight searching out rusts and lichened purples on its sandstone walls. She loved her Scottish home. In this house all her children had been born and from here they had flown like swallows to marry, or to perish. She sighed. Philip had looked his age when he left her this morning. He had not expected a summons from the south but could not ignore the crie de coeur from his Queen. He would be staying one night with Jean their youngest daughter in Perth and he had sent a message by boat to Edinburgh to tell Alastair to meet him at Stirling. The children would look after him, she was sure of that; even Alastair in his dreamy insolent way loved his father.

The thought did not banish the ache she felt in her heart. There was something at odds in Queen Joan's letter, something out of tune and mysterious in the words she had chosen, as if afraid to be frank. Alastair was well coached in the politics of the realm. Alastair would piece them together for him. She stood alone in her garden with the sun warm on her back, and shivered as if a cold breath from nowhere had touched her heart.

Three

Because she was French Bridget did not shy like a frightened mare from this shadow but searched for the cause of her fear. In these lawless days danger always lay await for the traveller. A resentful and starving peasantry seized and plundered. Clans of brigands, the "masterful beggaris" camped in the woods and preyed on single horsemen or the unguarded party. She knew that Philip with his armed band of Duffus stalwarts presented no tempting target to these foxes. It was when he entered the brambley thicket of Scottish politics that she feared for his safety.

Until the King's murder two years back, she and her husband had enjoyed his friendship and that of Queen Joan. Philip was fifteen years older than the King and the two might never have met but for a troubadour who sang to the young James of feats of arms at the bloody fray of the Red Harlaw. The King was in England then, prisoner of King Henry IV, and thirsty for news of his beloved Scotland. Three verses in the minstrel's song told of the fight between Philip Hogeston and the ranks of the clan MacLean. That tale of desperate courage so impressed the young captive that, thirteen years later, when he arranged his triumphant return to his country and to his throne, he asked for Philip and Bridget to attend him on the borders of his realm with others who shared his favour. They met at Coldstream in the valley below the Cheviots, where, to the blast of hunting horns and the tinkle of ice in the swollen river, Philip Hogeston was dubbed Knight by his royal master. Queen Joan took to the quiet Scot and his French wife and entertained them at Edinburgh, at Linlithgow and at Stirling. With King James's murder came anarchy. His son was a minor and the land was being quickly torn apart by two men, Crichton and Livingston, who each claimed to be Regent. In their struggle for possession of the boy King the country teetered on the brink of civil war.

Bridget thought of the letter that had arrived ten days before from Queen Joan and which commanded Philip's help. Its message was ambiguous. To her it suggested that the Queen had found herself a protector at last in James Stewart, Black Knight of Lorn. She remembered him as the handsome, chivalrous though rather ineffectual lord of western lochs and islands and loyal, like all Stewarts, to the dynasty of Robert the Bruce. Philip had put a different interpretation on the Queen's letter. He heard only her cry for help and was convinced that she was a prisoner of this Black Knight in his fortress at Dunstaffnage. If he was right he was riding into danger, but a danger he could recognise and by his training and experience, overcome. If he was wrong, he was like a ship without a rudder, approaching a whirlpool of ambition, betrayal and deceit.

"Alastair must help him." She spoke aloud, willing her words to be heard by her youngest son in far away Edinburgh. Alastair will advise him, Alastair will know how things are with the Queen. Then she remembered with a pang of disquiet how things had been for Alastair before he left home, the reproaches, the wordy battles with his exasperated father and his final dismissal.

"Make your way in the world with the only thing you are well skilled in, argument," Philip had said to his lazy fledgling when he flew at last from the nest.

Helped by some influential people but most of all by his gift of the gab the boy had talked his way into the crown law department and after only a month's apprenticeship he was, on probation, appointed an assistant legal adviser to the court of King James.

Plewlands was quieter but duller. There had been a flurry in the hamlet of Duffus when the woman Beatrix Sinclair announced her intention to join Alastair in Edinburgh. Bridget knew of this love affair and had tried to cool it down. In Beatrix she saw the local bitch in fast recurring heat, a prize attraction for all the lads in the village. Perhaps it was only to thumb her nose at Alastair's mother that Beatrix Sinclair set sail for Edinburgh but whatever reason the heave and thump of the little vessel as it lifted to the running sea had been too much for her. Mal de mer overcame her mal de coeur. She begged to be put ashore and was back in Duffus almost before she was missed, angry with herself, with Alastair and most of all with his mother.

As Bridget climbed the steps she wondered what sort of girl Alastair would marry. He was their heir and his father expected him to choose a wife wisely. Bridget was more tolerant. She drew the line at the Sinclair creature but made allowances for his youth. Few of his kind married before they were twenty-five, preferring first to rut with the stags. Her attitude had been quite different with the girls, Catherine and Jean, who, thank God were now married. Girls are no less adventurous and she was glad they were both mated and wed. "Time enough to have adventures from the safety of your marriage bond," she had told them, but what lass of sixteen could ever wait so long. She supposed the truly virtuous were hard to find outside a monastery, or even inside from the tales one heard, and all just a trifle dull. Youth fled too fast and virtue was a splendid garment, for old age. She stood on the topmost step and shook out her auburn hair. The lawn glowed beneath her like an eastern carpet and beyond the garden wall with its pointed gate she could see Mark lighting sulphur candles among the apple trees. He was younger than his father had been. She considered him carefully. I could improve his French as well, before Philip returns, if I really want to, she thought and as she stepped out of the sunlight into the cool shade of the hall her body gave a tiny answering shudder. She smiled. When she ceased to be flattered by a healthy young buck with bold and inquisitive eyes she would consider herself old. But that was not yet or now.

Four

Drunk from the Firth of Forth wind lurched round the castle rock, stumbled into the Grassmarket and spewed its bellyful of rain over streets and houses. A nightwatchman sheltered in the mouth of a vennel. He was cold and his feet were wet. He couldn't mind a worse summer. He knew the old castle town, its closes and its tall shaughly houses better than he knew his own poxy face. But tonight the streets were black empty corridors swept by the north wind. He thought to himself, "A thief maun be a feel tae plowther aboot on sic a night." The thought pleased him but nothing else did. It was after midnight and on any normal morning so near to midsummer the castle up there would be visible against a slow dawn. Mid-summer! What a wash out that had been. He shrugged his heavy coat close to his neck and remembered the feasting and the fun and the boozing of other midsummer nights, and the wenching, aye, especially the wenching. Christ, there was a bloody hail-storm this year with stones the size of peas, hard enough to hurt and mak the randiest wench pull doon her skirts and rin for hame. He heard a hammering, muffled by the gale, but near enough and he pressed back into the darkness of the archway. The hammering started again and, gripping the only weapon he was allowed to carry, a quarterstaff, he scurried out of the vennel, up the street and peeked anxiously into the darkness of the next close.

A man who looked like a sailor with a pigtail and bare feet and thick sailcloth trousers, stood on the cobblestones and stared up at shuttered windows. He was a scrap of a man and the nightwatchman challenged him, "What the Hell di ye think yer daein knockin' up fowk at this time of morn?" The sailor turned, hesitated, then thumped on the door, louder this time. A window creaked and a voice thick with sleep shouted down, "What di ye want?"

"Alastair Hogeston?" called out the sailor. "I have a message for you from Plewlands." The window slammed shut. The sailor looked undecided then feet sounded on a stair and bolts were drawn. Held by its chain the door opened six inches and a pale face glowered out.

"A bloody time to get a man from his bed," said Hogeston and took the letter. "Wait here," he commanded and locked the door. The two men outside in the rain saw peeps of light appear through slats of the storm window and upstairs the little room warmed to a candle flame. There was a heap of furs on a low bed, a half empty skin of wine on a table, some mugs and a woman's clothes scattered on the floor. The man called Hogeston prodded the rugs.

"Ola, where is your purse?" Although he could not converse in Gaelic he used the word 'sporran' to annoy her, knowing that an Orcadian refuses to speak the Celtic language and cares nothing for those who do. An impatient jerk of the skins was all the reply he got. He laughed, picked up a leather bag from the dresser, opened the window and threw some coins into the street. The sailor scrabbled for them then vanished like a handful of leaves plucked up by the night wind. The watchman plodded his way up the street in search of shelter. Hogeston stood for a moment frowning at the letter with the Viking longboat on its waxy seal. Then he opened it and spread the parchment on the table beneath the candle flame. The woman snored softly. In every word he read, Alastair Hogeston heard the brisk military voice of his father:

Plewlands, 8th July, 1439

"To Alastair Hogeston, Assistant Legal Adviser to the Court of King James.
Alastair. I am journeying south with all speed in obedience to the command of Queen Joan who is the prisoner of the Black Knight of Lorn in his castle at Dunstaffnage. I hope you can bring me

news of the Queen and the boy King before I take counsel with Livingston at Stirling. Your mother sends you her love.

Philip Hogeston."

A sleepy voice came from the bed.

"You will catch your death of cold standing there. What are you doing? Come back to bed." Alastair ignored her, frowned and re-read the letter. "I have a message from my father, Ola. He was, or hoped to be in Stirling yesterday. God damn that sailor for arriving late. I shall have to meet him before he rides into Lorn."

"What about me?" The woman sat up and the fur round her shoulders pulled her raven hair close to her cheeks.

"Do you expect me to stay here alone while you stravaig about after your father? He can fend for himself that one. From what you have told me, he has spent precious little time worrying about you these five years." Hogeston cut her short.

"He has asked for my help and it's seldom he does that. Find yourself another man if you get tired of your own company." He strode from the room and called loudly.

"Fraser, Kenneth Fraser." A young man with a curly mop of fair hair clattered up from below.

"Saddle the horses. We are for Stirling Castle," said Hogeston.

Fraser looked at his master and at the girl in the bed.

"You and her?"

Alastair snorted. "You and I, Fraser. I have to meet Sir Philip." Hogeston pulled off his night shirt. "Ola, where is the oil?" he asked.

"Why?" she countered, pouting as she watched him fumble about the room. "Is it really your father you are seeing or are you rutting off to another bed and another woman?" He picked up a small ornamental ivory tusk from the dresser and threw it on top of her knees.

"Use this until I come back to you," he grinned. He found the pot of spice oil and slapped some under his armpits and between his legs. When he had dressed, cap on head, booted, sword buckled to his side, he looked down at her. "Ola," he said softly, "I shall be gone a week or more. I have to take Fraser with me. You had best move to your sister's home." Dark eyes stared back from under long eyelashes.

"I have to take Fraser with me," she mimicked. "To stop him sleeping with me I suppose. Go to Hell Alastair Hogeston." One eyelid drooped in a half wink as she slid on to her stomach and cuddled the soft down of an eiderbag. Alastair looked at her shape beneath the furs. He stooped and gently gripped the small arch between her thighs. The girl drew in a breath.

"That can wait," he said. He placed two gold coins on the pillow in front of her eyes.

"And that is to keep it from wanting." He ran his fingers through her long thick hair, pulled on his coat and left the room. Ola lay quite still. She heard the door leading to the stable slam shut, and, after a few minutes, the clatter of hooves. She sighed cosily and wormed her body into the heap of fur and down. She thought of Hogeston and smiled, remembering how she had first met him. She had been standing on the swaying deck of an Orkney boat in the harbour of Leith. On the jetty a man was arguing with the captain. He was well dressed in grey broadcloth and wore a silver chain over a black silk jabot. He was hatless and the evening sun changed his long chestnut hair to copper. A handsome fellow he was, and an angry one.

"The woman asked to be put ashore at Aberdeen," the captain was explaining. "She told me to tell you she couldn't face another hour on the boat, not even with you at the end of her journey. It had nothing to do with me. She was plain miserable and sick." Ola had picked up her bags and timed her walk down the gangway just as the boat dipped sharply on the swell. She landed with a rush against the hard young body of the angry stranger. He took her assault well, steadying himself against a bollard, supporting the girl on his chest with one arm around her waist. She remembered, with a giggle, the bellow of laughter from the boat's captain and his jibe at Alastair. "For a landlubber you're a sprightly lad. You've lost one, but by God, you've found a better!" That was two months ago. She fell happily asleep.

Five

Dawn was a slow greying in the north east and a soaking of heavy rain. As the sky paled to yellow behind the Pentland hills Hogeston and Fraser rode by the palace of Linlithgow where candles peeped from high windows. Alastair pulled his bonnet over his ears. Since he left Edinburgh he had turned over in his head the string of possibilities which his father's letter required him to consider and thoughts recurred which evoked a tingle of fear. How much did his father understand about the struggle between the Regents Livingston and Crichton and what did he know of Queen Joan and Stewart of Lorn? As a legal adviser to the Court of the young King, Hogeston was well aware of the deadly rivalry that determined every action of Crichton in Edinburgh and Livingston in Stirling. Since the murder of King James and the untimely death of Archibald Douglas these two men had contested for the custody and control of the boy James II and ipso facto for the mastery of the Kingdom. But now Queen Joan, the royal widow, had thwarted them both by marrying James Stewart of Dunstaffnage, the Black Knight of Lorn. Alastair Hogeston knew that unless Livingston controlled the King, his grip on the Estates and his hold over the powerful nobles would quickly slip. He did not know how much of this intrigue was common gossip outside the bands of self-seekers who had settled, like leys in barrels of fermenting ale, around the Regents in Edinburgh and Stirling. What did his father know of the scheming politics of the Earls? Did he even know that Queen Joan had remarried? For if he did not know that, he was sailing into the vortex of a political storm in the centre of which was Livingston, greedy for power and totally ruthless.

At the back of Alastair Hogeston's mind a grub of self-recrimination began to squirm. As a boy he had often been punished or reproached by his father for sloth and for his unpunctual ways and he remembered his last meeting with Sir Philip so vividly that it brought out sweat in his armpits. For once Kenneth Fraser had failed him. There had been a loud rattling on his door which Alastair had heard only through a headful of wine, then his father's clipped voice.

"Not in is he, then I'll use his rooms to change my claes."

Alastair had leaped from bed and stood, six feet of total nakedness, hair uncombed, mouth open, before his father. Sir Philip took in the scene in one astonished glance, the mugs on the floor, the rancid smell of sweat and spilled drink, the heaps of clothes, and the faces of the two girls, big-eyed and curious, peeking above the furs on the bed.

"You fornicating waster," he roared. "I expected you to meet me two hours ago at the pier of Leith, and I find you in bed with not one, but two prostitutes." He raised his whip to lash his son's face, then slowly brought it back to his side, turned and strode from the room. Alastair heard him shout to Fraser to bring him his horse then the sound of hooves in the cobbled yard. Hogeston had stood and stared at the door feeling fresh sweat break out on his palms. The girls in his bed broke into giggles.

"Christ," he said, "Why is it I fear him so much yet forget to do his bidding?"

And now, riding head into the wind he thought "Holy Mother of God, he'll think I've done it again. Damn that boat for arriving late." He knew then that, hard as he might ride, Sir Philip would not wait for him and he had sunk even lower in his father's estimation.

The two horsemen rode into Stirling at noon and made for the house of James Maclehose, Signet to the Crown, a legal acquaintance if not a close friend of Alastair. He welcomed the pair cautiously but with courtesy and invited them to take dinner with him.

"Weel ma loon, ye've nae come ridin' through the glaur in the sma' oors tae speer hoo weel I am. Whit is it ye are after? Come on, oot wi' it!" Alastair pulled the letter from his pouch and handed it to the older man.

"This arrived before dawn today. It came by boat from the north and probably because of the gales it came late." Maclehose took the letter to the window and read and re-read the message.

"Aye. Weel noo. Aye. I can see why ye mounted up sae early. There could be a deal that your father kens naething aboot. Aye, ye're richt. Ye are a day late laddie. Sir Philip had conversation wi' Livingston yesterday and rode frae Stirling immediately. So much I ken and the rest I can find oot." He rang a small shrill bell and a servant appeared.

"Tell Alexander I want him here," he said. Then to Hogeston, "If your father is acting on Livingston's suggestion he could be in a peck o' trouble. Livingston is nae the man to miss an opportunity like this ane," and the little man waved Sir Philip's letter in Alastair's face. "He would do a great deal to grab the wee King and I am beginning to guess what he has told your father. I'll be far wrong if he has said a word to him aboot Queen Joan's marriage to the Black Knight." A thin figure in hodden grey appeared as if from nowhere in the room beside them.

"Find oot what Governor Livingston said to Sir Philip Hogeston yesterday," said Maclehose. The man he addressed shuffled his feet and looked almost in apology at the ground. In a voice so soft as to sound like a woman's he said, "Sir Philip has been sent tae his death. He is to be killed by a black knight in Lorn. The murder of a Queen's messenger will gie Alexander Livingston the excuse he wints tae march on Dunstaffnage and snatch the King." No one spoke. Alastair found himself staring amazed at this colourless man. Maclehose said sharply, "You say he is tae be killed by a black knight in Lorn. What you dinna say is The Black Knight of Lorn."

The man's eyes lifted quickly to engage the speaker then rested again on the floor.

"A black knight in Lorn is whit I said."

"Come man you talk in riddles," broke in Alastair. "His name then."

There was a silence, then from the grey man, "Ma freen, you are impatient and I dinna trust impatient men. But Alastair Hogeston, it may interest you to ken that the man who is engaged tae murder your faither is James Stewart of Badenoch." Hogeston was surprised and nettled. "You know my name although I have never met you and you refer to an adventure in the life of my father which I supposed was known to very few." He turned to James Maclehose. "I have heard my mother speak of the curse which James Stewart, third son of the Wolf of Badenoch hurled at my father at Lochindorb. Who is this fellow who knows so much? Can he be trusted to speak the truth?"

Maclehose placed a hand on Hogeston's arm and warned him with a look. "Thon is nae question you should ask," he said. "Alexander never speaks but to tell the truth. James Stewart of Badenoch, now of Garth Castle, is kent as 'The Fierce Wolf' and a man to reckon wi'. He is Livingston's hired killer and his work is as deadly as it is horrible. Noo if the information you have been given is of value to ye, your informant's time is nae less valuable to him."

Alastair Hogeston pulled out his purse and laid a gold coin on the table. A pale hand, jewelled in rings, lifted it and the man in grey left the room almost as if he had never been. James Maclehose stepped to a dresser and laid two silver wine-cups on the table. "Ask nae questions and ye'll be telt nae lees," he murmured as he poured the red wine. "God laddie ye maun guard thon tongue of yours. Alexander Ghru's nae the man tae relish being caa'ed a leear. Noo, on yer horse and awa' tae the lands of Lorn if ye want tae find yer faither alive. That killer James Stewart is nae named The Fierce Wolf oot of courtesy. If ye are yer faither's son ye will ride like the wind but I wouldnae wager on yer success."

Alastair Hogeston and Kenneth Fraser very nearly did succeed. Changing horses whenever they could they rode by Strathyre to Lochearnhead. There they were told that a Queen's messenger and his troop of horsemen were but five hours ahead. Weary, they continued the chase. Beyond Dalmally with Loch Awe and the Pass of Brander in view two wolves loped off into the forest and a pair of hoodie crows flapped heavily away from a shallow trench on the hillside. The two horsemen turned off the path and looked down on the grey dead face and half eaten torso of John Sime the Duffus blacksmith. Alerted to danger they rode fast below Cruachan and at the Bridge of Awe came upon a scene of carnage. Quietly cropping grass by the swollen river was his father's horse, the red Viking ship of the Hogestons emblazoned on its trappings. They found the first of the corpses hanging by its feet from the stirrups of another horse. Two men lay dead on the bridge pierced through by arrows. Three others had crawled amongst the alder and died face down in soft green moss. On the far side of the bridge the earth was churned by hoofmarks and splattered by blood. A sword was plunged deep in a rotting tree-stump and gripping to its hilt was a gloved hand severed above the wrist. Sick at heart Alastair prized the fingers from their dead grip and pulled off the glove. On the third finger was his father's ring. They searched the banks of the river as far as Loch Etive and found another body wedged among driftwood in the flooded estuary. They waded in and pulled it to the bank. Alastair knew him at once as John Reid, the thatcher at Duffus and as they hauled him from the river the body stirred and Reid opened his eyes. Recognition dawned.

"Master Alastair," he croaked. "God bless you sir but ye are ower late." The eyes closed and they thought he was dead.

Fraser stripped off his own riding coat and wrapped it round the ice-cold man. They lifted him on to the back of a horse and walked it to the shelter of the trees. Reid revived a bit as whisky trickled over his tongue and he opened his eyes.

"I heard them when I was under the bridge. They took your faither to Dunstaffnage. James Stewart said that it would 'complete the evidence'."

"The Black Knight of Lorn?" asked Alastair.

"No master. Black he was, horse, armour and helm, but he was anither James Stewart, son of the Wolf of Badenoch. I heard your faither say so afore they rode at each other." The flat words of the informer rung in

Alastair's memory. "The man charged wi' the murder of your faither is James Stewart of Badenoch." And James Maclehose's additional information – "Stewart of Garth, yclept The Fierce Wolf."

"Come Fraser. Tie John Reid to the saddle and we shall ride to Dunstaffnage."

Six

Three hours later they reached the fortress. It was well sited on a seagirt slice of land which pointed like a dagger towards the Benderloch and was defended to the landward by a deep moat and draw-bridge. Gardens and arbours of willow and hazel protected by a low thick wall lay to the south beyond the moat. Seen from the east the castle reared its gigantic walls from the rock of the seabed and at high tide waves thrashed themselves against it in a frenzy of foam. They found the postern gate unguarded and rode almost as far as the moat before they were stopped by a shout from the yet beneath the raised draw-bridge. "State your business strangers, and throw your arms to the ground."

"I am Alastair Hogeston, legal adviser to the Court of King James. These are my friends and one is sorely wounded. I search for my father Sir Philip Hogeston, messenger to the Queen, foully attacked at the Bridge of Awe."

They waited on the far side of the moat while the rumbling of chains round a windlass preceded the slow lowering of the massive draw-bridge. The portcullis was not raised and the men dismounted to lead their horses in single file into the castle. A tall man in black leather greeted them.

"I am James Stewart, the Black Knight of Lorn, Master of Dunstaffnage. Accept your sword Alastair Hogeston, and my friendship. Follow me."

"Stay with John Reid, Fraser, and see that he is made comfortable and warm," said Hogeston and followed Stewart up into the keep. They walked along corridors, up stairs and into a small room high in a tower overlooking the sea. On a bed lay a man. His face was white, his eyes sunken and ringed by black circles and beside him a woman. Hogeston knelt by the litter. There was a flicker of recognition, then the eyes closed and only the small rise and fall of his chest told Alastair that his father lived.

"How did he get here and what became of his enemy?" he asked.

"All in good time," said Stewart. "First you must know that my wife Joan has sat in vigil here since he was taken to my castle. If he lives it will be her doing."

Alastair stood abruptly and looked down on the face of the woman by his father's side.

"Majesty," he said and bent his knee.

"You will be Alastair my friend Philip's surviving son." She spoke softly and her voice held a hint of the English court. Alastair reflected she could only be a few years his senior yet she was the mother of the King and had six daughters beside. Her late husband had named her "the fairest and the freshest flower," but the punishments she had ordered and the scenes she had forced herself to witness marked her face with tiny wrinkles, around the lips and by her eyes. In her voice was a forlorn sadness that echoed these things as well as the plight of her friend.

"Yes Majesty," replied Alastair. "Thank you for tending my suffering father."

"He does not suffer. He is beyond that."

"Then he will not recover?" asked Alastair.

"I did not say so," Queen Joan replied, "And I shall see to it he lacks for nothing in care and comfort."

Later, Stewart said, "Tell me what you know of this strange business Hogeston. What was your father doing in the lands of Lorn?"

Hogeston told him all he knew. He produced his father's letter and described the meeting with the spy in the Maclehose house.

"You say he came in peace and was ambushed at the Bridge of Awe on the instructions of Livingston of Callander," said Stewart. "That tallies in part with what Queen Joan has told me although it was without my knowledge that she sent for your father. Nor, apparently did she see fit to tell him she was wife to the Black Knight of Lorn." The Black Knight smiled grimly. "That omission may yet cost your father his life. He is mortally wounded Hogeston and is not expected to live. He was carried by horsemen to the gate of my castle and dumped within the garden wall."

"There was no message, no explanation?" asked Hogeston.

"None," he replied. "And from the sound of your story none was intended. I shall scour Lorn tomorrow for these men – with little hope of finding them for they will have left my territory already if they are wise. I doubt the truth of your story. I do not disbelieve you, but I cannot easily imagine Alexander Livingston of Callander stooping to such depths of deceit and treachery. We shall talk more of this but now I must speak with the Queen."

Alastair watched them leave. The man was a typical aristocrat, with that ingrained faith in the code of chivalry which denied the existence of traitorous feelings in others of his rank. Livingston of Callander was an Earl and so his honour could not be impugned. Queen Joan might think otherwise thought Alastair. After his experience in Maclehose's room and at the Bridge of Awe, he had no such fine illusions, but the cunning Regent could yet get off with his honour and more important to him, with the King.

On that July evening, life slowly flowed back into the maimed body of one man and, as slowly, ebbed in cold sweat through the pores of another. When morning dawned over the mountains of Argyll the thatcher of Duffus was dead and the master of Plewlands had taken his first short step towards recovery. The sight of Alastair had given him hope. He had lived during the night with the souls of his dead sons slain many years back on the Field of Harlaw. He smelled again the stench of blood, heard the clash of Highland broadswords on Lowland armour and the terrifying scream of the pipes. His heart pounded with dread when two boys on ponies shouted to him, "We are here to help you, father," and the battle became a nightmare as Hector MacLean's barefooted swordsmen encircled his sons. He relived his hacking, thrusting, desperate fight to save them. He felt again the weight of their young corpses across his legs and saw their sightless eyes stare into an eternity he suddenly feared. He cradled them in his arms that long pale June night in the wake of battle when both armies, aghast at the carnage, fell apart like wild dogs to lick their wounds. As morning stole into that tower room in Dunstaffnage Castle the dead took their departure and in their place came the beautiful face of Bridget his wife.

Heavy rain from the sea drenched two other men who lay close to death on the shore of Loch Etive. Struck by arrows in the ambush on the bridge over the river Awe, Peter Grant and Percy Fowler pitched from their horses into the swollen river and were carried swiftly to the loch. The tide swept them north away from their searching enemies and later from their searching friends. Aeneas Macdonald, a herdsman, found them, made them a litter and carried them on his ponies to his croft in Dierdre's glen. He hid them in the straw when Stewart of Garth and his men rode up the loch looking for survivors of the Duffus troop. Stewart was certain that Philip Hogeston would die in Dunstaffnage and become part of the damning evidence Livingston would use to build his case against the Black Knight. The son of The Wolf wanted no living soul left to confound that evidence. But Peter Grant, Sir Philip's captain of troop, escaped his net and was helped by the folk on Loch Etive's shore north to Glencoe and thence by Glen Albyn to Moray where he told the tale of the massacre of his Duffus lads to their wives, sweethearts and bairns and of the murder, as he supposed, of his master, to Lady Bridget Hogeston of Plewlands.

Queen Joan, a realist accustomed to dereliction of honour by ambitious men, could not convince her new husband that Alastair was more than likely correct in his assertion that Livingston, co-Regent of the Realm was personally involved in this sordid intrigue and murder. Nevertheless, the lord of Dunstaffnage Castle was as good as his word and flung his considerable energy and knowledge of his territory into the hunt which followed for Stewart of Garth.

"Lorn," he explained, "Is a land of long sea lochs, high mountains and few passes. Dunstaffnage is linked to Inverary only by Glen Aray in the south-west. By Glen Orchy a troop of horse may ride north-east to Rannoch and a fair track as you know, Hogeston, leads east to Stirling by Crianlarich or south to Loch Lomond and Dunbarton. But all these routes must first traverse the Pass of Brander." So, to that narrow gorge flanked by Loch Awe and Ben Cruachan rode Hogeston, Fraser and a small band of scouts under the Black Knight of Lorn. A drearier place it would have been impossible to find on that rain soaked July when Ben Cruachan was striped by white cascades pouring from its precipitous slopes into Loch Awe, torrents which changed the path that clung to its shore into a river of dangerous depths and slippery footholds. A small squat out-post of rough hewn stone guarded the far end of the pass, manned constantly by a garrison from the castle. They reported they had seen no band of horsemen ride east since the Queen's messenger had stated his business four days ago.

"That was my father and the Duffus troop," said Alastair. The Black Knight was surprised, so sure he had been that the raiders were ahead of him. They turned west at daybreak. The lord of Lorn told the captain of the fort to hold the narrows against Stewart of Garth should he attempt the pass at any time and at the Bridge of Awe Hogeston and Fraser parted company with their host to search the south shore of Loch Etive. Stewart of Lorn would scour his lands and send a horseman after them if the enemy were sighted. Four days had passed since his father had been dropped like a gralloched stag at the gates of Dunstaffnage and Alastair was afraid all trace of the men from Garth would soon be washed from sight by the rain from the sea. But in Glen Etive they found their spoor. A fisherman on the loch had seen a band of horsemen searching the shore. He had pulled his skiff into the mist for they were armed and strangers. That night Fraser and Hogeston lay in a byre beneath Ben Starav. Their hopes were high and early next morning they came to the meadows of Dierdre and listened to the tale the herdsman told.

Seven

The croft of Aeneas MacDonald snuggled into the shelter of a straggling wood. Solitary stunted pines, blown into strange shapes, crouched on the slopes of the mountain and the less adventurous willows, alders and scrub-oaks clung to a burn that tumbled from distant corries. The buildings were circular walls of stone and lime roofed by turf and thatched with reeds. As if they had been there for ever they grew out of a flat shelf of ground formed by years of flood from the heart of Stob Ghabhar. Between the croft and the burn a few rigs of barley and oats stood green, waiting for summer warmth and a cockrel strutted nervously among his scratching hens. A man came to the door when Hogeston and Fraser reached the ford, a herdsman, a Hillman, strong, stocky and bandy-legged with a black beard and a long chin. He stood and watched them, a broadsword across his shoulder, as they urged their horses into the river.

"Come no closer," he shouted in Gaelic, "until you tell me who you are and what you want."

Kenneth spoke to the man in his own tongue then they rode their mounts across the stream and up to the croft through the growing corn. He stood at his door and glowered at them.

"What has become of the civility and the welcome we expect from Clan Donald?" asked Alastair.

The herdsman did not understand what Hogeston said but he recognised the authority in his voice and his truculence left him. Fraser repeated the question in Gaelic.

"Sirs," said the herdsman. "Forgive me for being ill-mannered but I have suffered a great grief and I am suspicious of strangers. My cattle have been stolen and my women folk abused."

Fraser translated this speech and then said to the man, "We search for a band of murderers. They are Stewarts of Garth. Were they the men who did these things?"

"They talked little but by their speech they could have come from Strath Tay and Garth was spoken of."

From the house, a thin woman in a grey woollen dress and shawl appeared and stood beside him. She did not speak but looked at the strangers with wary eyes.

"This is my wife Agnes," explained the man. "I am Aeneas MacDonald and you are welcome." Alastair acknowledged the woman.

"Can we help you Aeneas MacDonald?"

Without a word the woman motioned him into the croft. They stooped under the low lintel and entered her kitchen where fire glowed softly from a hearth in the middle of the room and a black pot steamed on its chain. Two doors led off, one into the byre which was empty and the other into a small bedroom. The kitchen was simply furnished. Three chairs stood round a rough table and two small stools nestled beside a box-bed. In the other room someone was crying but the weeping stopped when they came through the door. Agnes MacDonald lifted a heap of clothing from the table to the bed.

"Sit ye down friends," said Aeneas. "Wife, gie the strangers a bowl of soup."

Agnes gave her husband a hard look then bent to do his bidding.

The sobbing began again and Hogeston said to Fraser, "Ask her if she has a child that is sick and offer your help. You have boasted often enough of your skill in herbal remedies."

Agnes MacDonald straightened her back when Fraser spoke to her. She was a tall woman with a hard and bitter face.

"It is Eilidh that cries in there," she said. "She is scarcely fourteen and her weeping has not ceased since these accursed pigs departed. You cannot help her. Her malaise was caused by men, many men. No man can cure her for no man sought to help her." She stared at her husband. There was a hush, then Aeneas burst out,

"For Jesus sake, Agnes, don't look at me like that. Guid kens I'm no a brave man but what could I have done against twenty? I had two men, sair smitten, hidden in the byre under the hay who were hunted by these wolves. 'Has anyone passed this way?' their leader asked me. 'No sir,' said I.

"'Then I shall look inside.' I tried to stop him. I was afraid he would find the men for if he had I would have been strung up by my neck for helping them. How was I to know his attention would be so taken up by my women folk? He hit me on the mouth with his gloved fist. Di ye blame me for running away? I didna ken they would rape as well as steal." He turned to his wife.

"You are lucky to hae your man alive and still able to work for you."

"My man?" Agnes MacDonald's voice was full of scorn.

"I no longer have a man."

Aeneas appealed to Hogeston and Fraser.

"As God is my witness," he cried. "I could have done nothing."

Hogeston interrupted him. "What is all this about Fraser," he asked impatiently.

"When I have the truth from them I will tell you," replied Kenneth grimly. To Aeneas he said,

"What have they done to your women, MacDonald, that makes your wife so angry and your child weep?"

Agnes retorted. "How does he know when he wasna there. That swinish brute came through the door and saw us huddling here. He called out, 'There are twa young pullets in here and an auld hen,' and two of his rogues pulled me out of the house. I fought them and they called on others to grab my legs. Then they held me to the ground and raped me. Morag broke loose and ran down the glen but the black brute mounted his horse and went after her."

The sobs of the girl in the other room became louder.

"They tied poor Eilidh to the floor here and rode her one by one until the child's body pleasured them no longer. He," she nodded at Aeneas, "He lay hiding by the burn while his women screamed."

"What happened to your other daughter, Morag?" asked Fraser.

"The Beast caught her and dragged her by the hair into the house, where he used her as they had used Eilidh and me."

"Where is she now?"

"She went yesterday to get help from women down the glen. Eilidh needs the care of friendly souls who have not seen what she has seen or known what she has suffered."

Of the two men, Kenneth Fraser was the more affected by MacDonald's story. Hogeston's professional training conditioned him to violence and depravity but Fraser was not so inured and the rape of the three women sickened and enraged him. He was impatient for revenge and was glad when Alastair Hogeston decided to follow the raiders north and search out their lair. Foul deeds were mounting and required retribution but Hogeston's legal mind insisted that first he must sight the enemy and identify him without a shadow of doubt.

Eight

North of Dierdre's meadows there was only one route between the mountains. The track ran by the river as far as Bauchaille Etive Mor, the Great Shepherd of Etive, which straddled the approach to the glen and watched all travellers with a granite eye. Beyond, there was a fork west to Glencoe, and south-east the loneliest trail in Scotland skirted the moor of Rannoch then crept past the Black Mount to Breadalbane and the fertile valleys of the Tay and the Earn. The Glencoe route led only to the valley of Clan Donald, into the fastnesses of Loch Leven and the Mamore mountains. A party of horsemen riding from Dunstaffnage to the Tay valley could have got there more quickly by the Pass of Brander. Where then was James Stewart going? Twenty miles to the north-east across the moor and beyond Ben Alder were the hills of Badenoch and it now seemed likely that the son of the Wolf must have a lair in these mountains.

Since the ambush at the Bridge of Awe rain had washed in from the Atlantic and burns and bogs were swimming in flood. It was not easy to follow the trail even of such a large body of horse, but once the direction was suspected it was a matter of plodding on hoping for occasional proof of their passing. The cattle they had stolen from Aeneas MacDonald left soft stinking turds, visible even after rain. The sky cleared and far to the west the gashed summit of Ben Nevis was dark against a golden sunset. They topped a ridge and in the hollow below them light flashed from the door of a cottage and thick white peat smoke floated from its chimney hole. A horse shifted stance in the lean-to and a voice full of melody sang a love song of Gaeldom.

"Man is that not a fine tune?" said Kenneth. They tethered their horses and walked towards the light. The hut was filled with smoke and in front of the blazing fire a man sat on a heap of heather roots, a skin of liquor beside him. Yellow light flickered on a beardless ruddy face as with eyes closed he poured out his heart in praise of his nut-brown maiden. A shaggy black and white terrier stared at them, head tilted and ears pricked, then barked suddenly and dashed for the door, hair a-bristle. The singing stopped and the man peered into the darkness outside.

"What is it Bogle?" he asked. He reached in the heather and grasped a short sword.

"Parley with him,' said Alastair and knocked loudly on the half open door. The barking increased and the voice inside shouted in the Gaelic,

"Come in slowly, unarmed or I'll chop ye like thistles."

Kenneth pushed open the door, stooped to enter and the terrier sprang towards him. The singer was on his feet his sword pointed belly high. Kenneth grinned and spread his hands.

"Would you slaughter two travellers who are lost and benighted on your accursed moor?" he asked softly in the old tongue. The man looked at them carefully, lowered his sword, then with a dramatic sweep of his left arm, bowed and said, "Enter my home then strangers. You are welcome to my fireside. Shut the door if you can or the licht will attract more of ye from the moor. I canna mind when this place has been so popular wi' the rag-tag o' Rannoch. Here, sit doon and dry yer claes. Hae a houp." He pushed the skin of liquor towards them.

"I am Kenneth Fraser and this is my master, Alastair Hogeston, lawyer in Edinburgh."

"And I," said the big man in the sibilant English of the Celt, "Am Somerled Cameron, herdsman and tacksman to the Badger. You can call me Sam."

"Who is the Badger?" asked Kenneth.

"Hoots man ye're an ignorant pair. The Badger, as all men should ken, is my Chief in Glencoe – Ian MacDonald – and if you should meet him you will understand why he is so called, the more quickly if you have the misfortune to disagree with him. He has the stealth of the

Badger, the night eyes of the Badger and the ferocity of the Badger."
He grasped the liquor bag and passed it to Alastair. "My oh my, but it's
grand company I keep. Hae a houp o' uisge beathe lawyer Hogeston."
Alastair took a long swig of the fiery whisky. It caught at his breath.

"Good stuff," he said.

"It should be," said Sam. "I made it myself!"

He laughed and broke into the song they had heard as they came
across the moor.

"In waking and in dreaming you're evermore with me."

Kenneth joined in the song.

"You're a fine ane," he said, "And ye keep a couthy hame."

"This is no my home, ye fool," Sam retorted.

"Na lad, my hame is where my lassie is and she's far awa'."

He broke into another love song,

> "When I'm lonely dear white heart
> Dark the night or black the sea
> May the light my foot finds
> Be a pathway to thee."

The whisky passed from man to man.

"We have been following the tracks of some horsemen," said
Kenneth presently. "They would have passed here by any chance?"

"Aye," said Sam. "Ye are well behind them and they had cattle wi'
them. It must have been near a week syne and a dour lot they were.
Devil a cheep of a greeting did I get from any of them. Their leader
was a big lout, thin and tall, with the coldest face I've seen on any man
– like his wife had kept it to herself for a month." He roared at his
own joke then broke into the baudiest song they had ever heard which
lasted as long as the singer could stay awake.

They saddled up at first light. Sam whistled shrilly and the dog
Bogle leaped off over the moor.

"He kens where the beasts are," explained Sam. "Maist are back at
the fold – the grass is sweet and thick down there by the loch – but a
few who have calved late are up here on the hill."

The trail they followed was little more than a deerpath. It edged past crags, skirted mossy hollows, leaped over torrents and at last slipped and twisted its way down from the moors through groves of alder and mountain ash and solitary stunted pines. They rode slowly for half the day, moving the cattle off high pastures they shared with red deer down to the grassy meadows of the valley. It was mid-afternoon before the three horsemen and the dog dropped beneath the cloud and saw dark green forest and the distant grey sheen of Loch Ossian. When the fold came into sight Sam's chatter stopped.

"The cattle are gone," he exclaimed. "That crowd of brigands have lifted the herd." The kindly expression on his red face changed and his eyes were wild and angry.

"If they have touched Mary with their dirty hands I'll slaughter the lot of them or die working at it." Sam scanned the far shore. A wisp of white smoke spread out over the tree tops.

"God be praised, she's safe. That surely is all that matters."

They rode fast through the forest and forded the river Ossian as it poured from its loch. Lush meadows a-gleam with buttercups spread down to the waterside and where the pines marched forward the cottage stood. A plump young woman with dark eyebrows and solemn eyes opened the door and smiled when she saw Sam. A baby cried in its crib and the smell of new-made scones and oatcakes filled the tiny house, as neat as Sam's hill-sheiling had been disorderly. Sam whisked her off her feet and gave her a hug.

"Somerled what ails you? You'd think you'd been away the whole year and not just a week or two. Put me down you big fool."

"She calls me Somerled when she is angry," laughed Sam.

"Woman, I'm always glad to see you and doubly glad today."

He told her of the theft of his cattle and of his fears for her safety.

"The rascals must have been too busy driving off your wild hill stirks to remember about me," she said quietly.

"Do you know these men?" asked Alastair.

"We have seen them move about the bealachs," said Mary. "They come from the north beyond the long loch. Sam has watched them riding on the shore of Loch Ericht."

"They raped three women in Glen Etive," said Kenneth fiercely. There was a silence, then Sam spoke quietly and with passion, "Bad luck on the bastards then. The MacDonalds won't waste pity when they catch up with them. Mary, I can see your father's face when he hears of this. Was it Aeneas' wife and quines?"

"Aye," replied Kenneth. "We had enough ado to stop him riding with us. Aeneas was after blood."

"Indeed, indeed, Aeneas is a great talker but not much of a do-er," was Sam's remark. Alastair was listening to the conversation with only one ear. His thoughts had raced ahead.

"It would be rash to tackle twenty men with three," he said, "But if Glencoe will rise –"

"Nae 'but' aboot it," retorted Sam. "They may already be on the way."

Alastair pondered this, then turning to Fraser he said, "To take them by surprise we must know exactly where to find them. If they are in the north they can be taken also from the north. I don't know how well recovered Peter Grant can be but he will waste no time in returning well armed and with horsemen. If we could all strike at once we could wipe James Stewart and his band from the face of Scotland."

"Ach ye talk like a lawyer. That's for the future. In the meantime what about my cattle?" asked Sam. "I am for pressing on now and stealing them back."

"We could try that," said Alastair. "We must locate Stewart anyway. He could be in Laggan or even in Badenoch. Although there is no one now in Lochindorb, the Wolf had other lairs and his whelp will know them all."

They sat down to a meal of porridge, trout, oat-cakes and cheese followed by new baked bannocks filled with blueberries and honey and to Fraser and Hogeston the feast was welcome for they had eaten little since they had left Glen Etive.

Nine

The men stood at the door of the house. Sun turned the morning mists to dew and lit sharp stars on the quiet face of Loch Ossian. Robins were calling to cross-bills in the pine forest and a wedge of wild-duck swooped over the water to vanish in the rushes. It was hard for Alastair to believe that since he had left Ola cocooned in eiderdown in the house at the Grassmarket, eight men had died, three women had been raped, a man, his wife and baby robbed of their living and all because of an ancient hate which had first blazed before he was born. He often wondered at the strange happenings which had involved his father in the island fortress of Lochindorb. His father had never talked of them. He knew that somewhere a written confession lay hidden. So much his mother had told him. From Peter Grant, Sir Philip's squire and friend, he had learned of the desperate fight on the steps of Elgin Cathedral on the night of its destruction by fire when his father had been captured and imprisoned by the Wolf of Badenoch in his castle at Lochindorb. That was the first oddity of behaviour that marred an uncritical acceptance of his father's strange sojourn at Lochindorb. Alastair wondered at the Wolf's decision to capture the young priest when he could so easily have had him slain as he fought alone outside the locked doors of the Cathedral. Peter Grant who had been a slaughter-man in the castle kitchens told him something of the two years his father had spent there. It was plain that he had enjoyed complete freedom. He had been a novice in the Cathedral when he was taken and during his months in Lochindorb Castle he acted as priest to the Wolf's family. Even Peter Grant's respect for Sir Philip Hogeston failed to give credibility to the tales he told of his master's adventures but instead built up a picture of a man who was larger than life.

So thought his youngest son. Through the web of capture, violence and escape ran the weft of duplicity and the suspicion of illicit love. The name of Mariota Athyn mistress of the Wolf, inflamed Alastair's imagination not by what he was told by his mother and by Peter Grant but by what was unsaid and left in question. He suspected that behind Peter's tales of bravado lay another story of intrigue and lust. Alastair Hogeston had never seen James Stewart, third son of the Wolf but the curse he had hurled at his father, Philip Hogeston, on a day of tension and decision at Lochindorb, sent a shudder through his body. The fearful revenge taken upon Philip Hogeston at the bridge over the river Awe shouted of hatred founded on deep and unforgivable insult. James Stewart was sixteen at the time of the disruption of his family. There had been a violent scene during a night of feasting and drinking which ended in a challenge flung at the Wolf by Philip Hogeston. The next morning in full view of her son James, Mariota Athyn was escorted from her home by her husband to vanish for ever from James' life. The boy had been there in the great hall of Lochindorb Castle when the Wolf had accused Mariota and his captive priest of – witchcraft! For years Alastair Hogeston's imagination had fed on these scenes. His pubescent dreams were filled with the physical presence of a woman's body, withdrawn from his touch and half-concealed by silken hair the colour of ripe wheat. Her name was Mariota. The flood of guilt which accompanied these dreams was expurgated by the nightmare appearance of his father in the black habit of a monk. Hogeston wondered what he would have done had he been James Stewart. Would he have sustained over the years a hate so intense that annihilation was the only possible way of wiping the slate clean? Philip Hogeston might yet live but his death from the wounds inflicted by his enemy was more than likely. He tried to picture his father as a younger man and saw only his mother Bridget de Dreux and her despair if she learned of Sir Philip's death.

A long skein of geese gaggled their way overhead, etched in flight against pale green uplands and the distant crags of Ben Alder. Hogeston broke a twig from the rowan bush by the door and traced a map on the ground.

"We are here at Loch Ossian," he said. "To the east is Ben Alder. Beyond the Ben the Loch of Ericht slices the hills thirteen miles into Badenoch and the valley of the Spey. Glen Laggan from Lochaber to Kingussie is beyond, and farther to the north, the Monadhliaths, and the Pass of Corrieyairack to Glen Albyn. Here, the Great Glen runs like an arrow from the sea to Inverness and the Moray Firth, and is the main route by track and ship to the Earldoms of the north. What better place for that nest of vipers than here –" He traced a circle with its centre north of Ben Alder. Somerled Cameron stood back a pace and looked at Alastair with respect.

"Man," he said, "I've lived all my life in Glencoe and the Rannoch and if ye'd speared at me what was behind the Ben there," he pointed to the rest of the horizon, "I would have telt ye water kelpies and fairies! How di ye ken all this?" He passed his hand over the rough map on the grass.

"I spent my early years riding the Long Glen from the western sea and back with merchants from France," said Hogeston. "They traded clothing, silks and swords for our hides and salt salmon. The trade was good and continuous but it had to run the gauntlet of the English pirates, the sea robbers of the Western Isles and marauders from north and south of the Great Glen." He placed the point of his stick on the ground. "The bridge of land here between Loch Oich and Loch Ness suits the brigands from the hills. They swoop from the bealachs, cut out the pack horses, slaughter the riders and disappear into the mists of the Corrieyairack. I was once on a punitive ride with the Earl of Moray and fifty horsemen. We struggled up and over the high Corrieyairack, met no one, saw nothing and returned empty-handed by the pass of the Slochd. But I learned much about that empty wilderness of the Monadhliaths where a whole army could hide and where herds of cattle could vanish without trace. I know that country. It was made for men like James Stewart." Kenneth Fraser listened with attention.

"When I was a laddie I lived in a croft in Glen Truim," he said. "After my father died I was taken there by my mither to stay with my granny. I fished Loch Ericht and rode after stag on Ben Alder. There is a corrie – here." He knelt and laid a finger on the grass. "This is where the hinds foaled, fine upland country wi' a loch and sweet grass. Had there been a tree or twa I would have built a sheiling and fed my beasts well at the summer herding." Sam interrupted him.

"Aye and talking of beasts there is nae sense in wasting time if I am to fetch them back before they are slaughtered. Mary my lass, ye'll make your way this day with the bairn to Glencoe. Tell your father what is afoot."

"Who is Mary's father?" asked Alastair.

"The Chief of the clan," replied Sam proudly, "Ian MacDonald, The Badger. Tell him, Mary, that I have the friendship of two braw lads who are also hunting the one who calls himself The Fierce Wolf. Tell him what happened in the meadow of Dierdre to Aeneas' wife and quines."

"If you are to be away for some days," said his wife, "Why must I leave so soon?"

"Because I say so," he replied impatiently, then, "Mary, my love, if we succeed in taking my cattle off these men, we can expect them to follow us. I would sooner trust you and wee John to a pack of weasles than leave you to the mean anger of this James Stewart."

Ten

It was past noon when they turned their horses off the Labhair burn and rode for the Chumbann pass. The trail left by the stolen cattle was clear and the footprints of the raiding party indicated leisurely progress. They had almost a week's start and would not expect to be followed.

"Your beasts will be cropping the grass in the high corrie below Ben Alder," said Kenneth. "They have been herded through the Black Pass which means that Stewart's men have reached their hide-out from the north, the easier but the longer route."

Kenneth guessed that their camp would be above the loch, probably beneath the Garbh coire where they would be sheltered, watered and provided with an unobserved view of the whole valley.

"The loch is encircled by crags," he explained. "A small burn flows out of it to the north and the only other way into the valley is from the south over a high pass."

"Then that is the way we shall take," said Sam, "and we shall sleep the night in a cave above the head of Loch Ericht."

They toiled up a gorge that for a mile climbed steeply between towering sun-baked cliffs. Since they left the cottage by Loch Ossian, Sam's little terrier, Bogle, had run with them but when they reached the first of the rocks Sam picked him up and settled him in a saddle-bag. He was panting in the heat.

"I don't know why you took that wee beast with you," said Kenneth.

"Not for his company," replied Sam, "Although he is as good a friend as any man I know. I just ken he will be useful on this journey. He is a rare wee watch-dog. He seldom barks but he is aye alert and he is the finest herding dog I have ever owned."

In the shadow of the cliff, airs gusted from above and whipped a thousand particles of granite dust into their faces. The long descent down the Alder burn took them below the full fury of the wind and it was dusk by the time they reached the cave. Sam guided the horses to a grassy slope above Loch Ericht. The cave was draughty, the walls damp, but at the back was a pile of heather and bracken.

"Get some sleep now," advised Sam, "for we must be out of here as soon as the moon rises."

"I take it that your plan is to have us in position at the top of the south pass of the corrie by dawn," said Alastair.

"Long before then," Sam exclaimed. "There will be plenty light from the full moon that will shine into the valley from over our backs, bright enough I am sure to let us see where Stewart's men are camped, and where my cattle are grazing. We must be well into the Rannoch Moor by full daylight."

The climb up the steep slopes was difficult in the dark. The going became a little easier in moonlight and before she was a hands-breadth above the ridges of the south-east they had arrived at the summit of the pass and looked down on a loch in the middle of the mountain. They moved to the left holding their height and in the shadow of the crags peered into a deep cut in the mountain wall. It faced north and snow which had filled it from October to April lay untouched by the summer sun. At the top of this gully the moon gleamed on a huge cornice of melting ice hanging like the crest of a wave over the valley beneath. Down on the floor of the corrie the round humps of skin tents could be seen half a mile away four hundred feet below and on the slopes beneath them, the shapes of grazing cattle.

"Those are my beasts," whispered Sam.

"How are we going to drive them off without wakening the camp?" asked Alastair. Sam sat for a while casting around for inspiration.

"I'll tell ye how it is to be done," he said at last.

"I'll draw them back up the valley and when they are beyond that mark there," he pointed directly below, "you must start an avalanche."

"Just how do you propose we do that?" asked Alastair. Sam uncoiled a long length of tow he had carried wound round his waist.

"Kenneth, you are the heaviest. You will climb to the top, there, and you Alastair will anchor yourself to a rock above him, there. When the time comes, Ken, jump on the overhang of ice and break it into the gully. If the rope holds, and it has held many a wild stirk, you will drop down safely through the cornice to the soft snow here below Alastair."

"With a lot of luck," said Kenneth in disbelief. "You dinna really mean that Sam?"

"I certainly do. There is a huge weight of snow in this gully that will break away from the rocks once that cornice falls. It will block off the valley below and we will be off with the beasts before anyone is the wiser."

"My God," swore Alastair, "Can you not think of a safer way than this. What if the rope breaks? What if Ken is smothered in the falling snow."

"What if the sky falls in! Damn it man what is life but a succession of risks and good luck." Sam slapped Ken on the back.

"You'll do it and you'll survive. Right!"

"Right," replied Ken but without enthusiasm.

"Before the snow settles we will meet where we first looked down into the valley and the beasts will join us before long. Remember Ken, don't start the snow-fall until you see the cattle pass the bottom of the gorge." Sam picked up the terrier.

"Now you will see what Bogle is worth. Good wee dog." He said in Bogle's ear, "Go and lead the cattle boy, herd them there," and he pointed up the valley with his right arm. "Off you go."

Away went the dog, scrambling and slithering down the slope in the moonlight toward the grazing animals. Kenneth tied himself securely to the end of the rope and crawled on his stomach across the cornice to the centre of the overhang. Alastair wrapped the other end of the rope round a spur of rock on the left hand wall of the snow gully above Kenneth, tested it, and then tied it tightly to himself. Far below, they saw the dog in amongst the beasts, biting at the soft skin above their hooves.

They could hear him whimpering gently. Their ears pricked, the cattle at first stood stock still and looked at their tormentor. Then the biggest in the group started moving slowly at first then faster towards the dog and others followed until the whole herd was on the run.

"Now," said Sam. Kenneth got to his feet and jumped up and down on the lip of the cornice. There was a "whoosh" as the long edge of ice and snow came away from the rock face. It hung for a moment then, with Kenneth still on top, it crashed into the snow gully. The rope tightened round its belay, held, and Kenneth, arms and legs thrashing to free himself from the falling snow, came penduluming across to safety directly below Alastair's perch. The "whoosh" was now a roar as the packed snow in the gully started to rush downwards. In two minutes the avalanche was over and the valley from the cliffs to the loch was blocked, covered feet deep in snow and rock.

"Quick now," said Sam. They ran the short distance, leaping and sliding on moss to the rim of the mountain where they had first looked into the corrie. Behind them, blowing, snorting cattle struggled up the slope in pursuit of Bogle, spurred on by the noise of the avalanche behind them.

"Now, was that not a neat night's work?" Sam said when they reached the cave above Loch Ericht. "Well done Ken. You got her going in fine style."

"Never again," said Kenneth rubbing his bruised legs and scratched chest. "What a bloody risk to take for fifteen black beasts."

"Ach it wasn't all that dangerous," said Sam. "Sure as God they will never know how the cattle have been taken from them. You can't have counted them right Ken. There are twenty if there is one!"

They drove the animals beyond the cave to the grassy shores of Loch Ericht. "Now boys for the long hard push across Rannoch to Laidon and Glencoe," said Sam. "And I am telling you it will be hard going on the worst bog you have ever seen."

Hour by hour they drove the cattle and when at last the sun scattered light over the edge of the world the crags of Alder had dropped out of sight behind the shoulder of Ben Pharlagain. "Give them a rest," said Sam, "and we can get out of the saddle for a spell. With any luck we have escaped unnoticed. For the past hour, since day break, they could have seen us from the Ben Alder pass but it would be hard for them to make us out because they would be looking straight into the rising sun."

"Is it more likely that they suspect nothing?" asked Alastair. "I pose this question for the rest of my plan will depend on it. If that nest of robbers in the Ben Alder corrie are unaware that anyone has penetrated their hiding place then we shall hold the element of total surprise when we come at them again, and that pleases me greatly."

"I am real pleased myself," laughed Sam. "Now let's get these beasts on the move. Glencoe is a fair step ahead and until this business is finished I'll not see Loch Ossian or Mary again."

Eleven

It was afternoon the following day when the three horsemen reached Glencoe and the herdsman's house at Achrambeithach. They were very tired but in good spirits. Night had over taken them at the head of Glen Etive where they herded the cattle into a dry stone fold, settled them and lay down beside them. Their black bodies took the chill out of the air and the strong sour stink of their breath clung to their clothes and to their hair.

Two of the beasts were lost on the way. One drowned in a bog below the Black Corrie. The other was crowded from the track in the ravine at the throat of Glen Coe. Its terrified bellow was cut off by the roar of white water when it struck the rocks and vanished in the torrent. At Achrambeithach Sam took time only to swill his face and hands.

"Look after these fine lads and my bonnie beasts," he told the herdsman. "I'm off to see MacDonald, and Mary." His eyes twinkled. "Nae doot her father will want to ken what his good-son has been daein. Clean yourselves and follow me doon tae the hoose."

The house, a two-storey building in squared grey stone, was quite different from the round-stoned, thatched cottages of the clansmen and was roofed in black Ballachulish slate. It stood among green meadows and looked as permanent in the landscape as the crags of Aonach Eagach. The horsemen saw farm buildings, a fold and a stable. The drizzle stopped when they came out of the cloud and under the grey shelf of the sky Loch Leven stretched to the west like a plate of polished pewter through the narrows of Ballachulish to Loch Linnhe and the ocean. Close to the shore, as motionless as toy galleons, lay three ships facing east in the ebb tide towards the vee in the glen where the horsemen stood. Hogeston and Fraser saw high curving prows, long low hulls, raked masts and sails tightly rolled to slanting booms. There was no movement on them but to the watchers the three war-boats, sleek and menacing, had a life of their own. They looked exactly what they were, swift merciless raiders of the western sea.

The riders tied their horses to the rail under an ancient oak in front of the chief's house. The door opened as they strode up the path and Sam came out clad in the red plaid of his wife's clan.

"Welcome! MacDonald, these are the men, Alastair Hogeston and Kenneth Fraser."

"Forgive me," said Hogeston as he bowed before the massive bulk of the Chief. "I have not the Gaelic but my friend has and will translate my speech into your tongue."

"No need," replied the Badger. "All here of any importance can talk in French. Je vous souhaite la bienvenue." He swung round to a group of men beside the fire and continued fluently, "I have the honour to introduce my kinsman Donald Balloch, nephew of Alexander Lord of the Western Isles." A large man lay back on a pile of rugs and skins. Not a muscle of him moved but in the firelight Hogeston saw eyes that studied him carefully. Behind the Islesman stood three others with the alert carelessness of trained guards, their hands hovering by their kirks.

"Do your duty, Somerled," said his chief. "Glencoe aye welcomes the stranger." Sam opened a door at the back of the big room.

"Mary lass, bring in the mead."

Mary Cameron carried in a tray with silver goblets and a tall flask of spirits.

"God be with you friends," she said quietly to Alastair and Kenneth, "and thank you." She poured the mead for the guests, her father, Donald Balloch, the watchdogs by the chimney, Sam and lastly for two young men who stood by the door.

"Malcolm Beg and Ranald Mor are you old enough to take liquor?" she asked. Above the murmur of talk Malcolm's reply was heard by everyone.

"Hold your tongue little sister and get back to the women." It was the angry voice of youth, the awkward tones of the boy reaching for manhood. Mary giggled.

"Laddie, wouldn't you just love to come with me."

"Haud your peace," said the other boy. "If you do not know how Malcolm feels you are either blind or stupid."

"Aye Mary," said her father. "If you can't see how it is with the boy don't cut him with your woman's tongue. Off ye go. And tell your mother to bring in the food."

Mary pulled a long face, dropped a curtsey to her father and swung her graceful form out of the room. In the pause that followed a voice came from the fireside.

"Speak up young MacDonald. What ails you? Cousin, is your son tongue-tied?" Donald Balloch swung his gaze on the boy Malcolm.

"Och," said his father, "the laddie suffers from a bad attack of calf love and he has had some news that disturbs him." He turned to Hogeston.

"Alastair Hogeston, can you enlighten us on the affair at the meadows of Dierdre?"

A young voice came from the shadows.

"Father, I speak for Malcolm and for myself. Is that dreadful deed to be spoken of so freely? Do we wash our linen in company? Surely the Clan council is the place to unravel this wrong."

"Guard your tongue Ranald. There is no better place to enquire into this business than in my own house and in the presence of cousin Donald." The chief turned towards the Islesman.

"It is your decision, MacDonald," came the reply.

"Come then Alastair Hogeston, let us have your story," said the Chief.

"To begin with," began Alastair, "you must have patience while I explain to you how and why I came to be there in Glen Etive. My father Sir Philip Hogeston of Plewlands was a friend and confidant of Queen Joan. At her command he rode into Lorn to seek her release and that of her son the young King, who he wrongly assumed were prisoners of the Black Knight of Lorn. He was ambushed at the Bridge of Awe by a knight in black armour, one James Stewart not of Lorn but the third son of the Wolf of Badenoch."

There was a rumble from MacDonald's throat, "I know the man," he said. "He calls himself The Fierce Wolf and seeks to settle Strathtay with his own sort. He has had words with McIver of Glenlyon. He is better known to his enemies as The Accused Whelp. But on with your tale."

"I arrived at the Bridge of Awe shortly after the ambush and found one man of Sir Philip's troop living. He told me before he died that my father, sorely wounded, was carried to Dunstaffnage Castle by James Stewart of Badenoch. He is there now, still alive I rejoice to say. Fraser and I together with Stewart of Dunstaffnage hunted the hills of Lorn for his enemy and at last found his trail leading up Glen Etive. Aeneas MacDonald had concealed my father's captain, Peter Grant and one other under straw in his byre. He tells me that Grant later reached Glencoe and may be well on his way home. Is that true?"

"Aye, we gave two men, Peter Grant and Percy Fowler an escort and a litter to see them back to Moray. They were sairly wounded but in a hurry to be home. They could not speak the Gaelic and were unable to tell us what had happened to them or to Aeneas and his women folk. What did happen to the women at the croft of Deirdre?"

"Stewart's men raped them," said Alastair.

"Sacre Coeur! Tell your story exactly as it was told to you," commanded the Badger.

"They forced Agnes to the ground first. Eilidh, they tied to the floor of the kitchen and raped in turn. Morag fled up the river. 'Leave her to me,' James Stewart cried and set off after her. He caught her, brought her back and all night had his way with her in her mother's bed. They left next morning and Aeneas was surprised his house was not burned to the ground. Stewart called to him as he left, 'I leave your house standing MacDonald so that I may have a love nest in Glen Etive." Raped though she was, Aeneas has Morag to thank for his life and his croft."

A boy's voice cracked through the silence. "And what lie does that remark conceal?"

"Only, I assume. That Morag had kept her head though her body was ravished and that thanks to her wits her father, mother, sister and home were spared," replied his father.

The men thought about this for a while.

"Aye," said Ranald, "Morag would rape easy."

Malcolm gave a cry of rage and threw himself at his brother.

"Take back that foul remark," he screamed.

"Hold your temper boy," roared his father. "Ranald leave this room and return only when you can control the acid in your tongue. And you, Malcolm, go to your mother. I will not have strife among brothers. No sons of mine will brawl in my company." He turned to Alastair.

"So Hogeston, however you interpret the actions of one young woman at Glen Etive, there is no arguing that three MacDonald women were raped by Stewart and his men in their own house in MacDonald country. Rape and maltreatment of his women folk no MacDonald can suffer without revenge. I will set my Clan on the heels of this James Stewart and his nest of vipers and will teach them a bloody lesson they will not forget – if any survive to have memory of it. Somerled, where do you say you found them?" Sam plucked a long burning brand from the fire and drew in charcoal on the hearth the location of the camp in the heart of Ben Alder.

"Twenty men you say?" said his Chief. "Twenty men it shall be then, and I shall lead them myself."

The man on the heap of skins by the fire sprang to his feet. Coiled on the hearth, only his plaid of green and his black beard had impressed. Now, a hush of admiration extinguished the talk. In a single smooth movement, over six feet of bulk and strength stood between them and the red glow of the fire. The two crusie lamps on the wall flickered. His shadow filled the room.

"Mount twenty of my bonnie men MacDonald and I too shall ride with you. My crews who remain can provision the galleys and I shall be back in four days with Stewart heads to nail to my masts and Stewart horses to fill my ships. Your twenty men shall match the twenty

Stewarts at Ben Alder and my twenty shall stand at the corrie mouth and see fair play." The giant tilted his head to the roof and a gale of laughter shook the house.

"Honour shall be served MacDonald and justice shall be seen to be done." Again a roar of laughter belched from the big man.

"'Twill be a lesson indeed to the Stewarts that it is as pleasant to open the jaws of a shark as to open the legs of a MacDonald woman against her will."

The men thundered their applause in a cheer that set the tallow candles quivering.

"Fetch food Somerled," cried the Badger, "and tell the women to bring more liquor." He threw peat and wood on the flames and sparks cracked like Chinese fireworks. Pee-wits rose afrighted by the sound of the ancient war-cries and, out on the quiet loch, the men manning the galleons heard, and laughed, and talked of the clash and blood of other battles.

Twelve

Through the mists and from beyond the rim of dark mountains dawn filtered into Glencoe. Alastair awoke with his head filled by the shouts and songs of the night and his mouth fouled by drink. He pulled hay from his neck and hair, sat up, and thumped his head on a wooden trough. A beast blew in the darkness and a shaft of light from the roof-hole played on the sleeping figure of Kenneth Fraser.

"Wake up for God's sake Fraser," said Alastair. "Your snoring will fleg the cattle."

He held his throbbing brow and wondered if ever again he could look on a flagon of mead. He shook his head and tried to arrange his thoughts.

"Kenneth, we are wasting our time here," he said. "We have no part in this clan feud. We shall not find James Stewart in the Ben Alder corrie. Some of his men perhaps, but the man I seek will have returned to the comfort of Castle Garth long before the MacDonalds swoop on his mountain lair. Ben Alder was only a base to which he withdrew after his attack on my father's men. By moving north he must have planned to confuse his pursuers, if any. He was not to know that Reid the thatcher or my father would live to reveal the real identity of the Black Knight at the Bridge of Awe. Think again of that ambush Kenneth. It has prepared the way for an assault by Livingston on Dunstaffnage. Stewart of Lorn is known as "The Black Knight", and a black knight attacked an envoy from governor Livingston to the Queen. An armed attempt to storm Dunstaffnage and snatch the Queen and the young King may already be under way, and my father as well as the King is in danger. It is with him I should be, and soon. All my instincts tell me that the massacre of my father's men was a deliberate part of Livingston's plan to march with apparent justice against Stewart of Dunstaffnage Castle. Give me water to wash and I shall tell the Badger I must ride south to Lorn."

Kenneth Fraser leant against the jamb of the open door and looked at his master.

"I have never told you this," he began quietly. His lean body was motionless, his hands were still.

"I am the son of Simon Fraser the smith of Invermoriston. I was nine years old when he was killed in battle and the town of Inverness was put to the sword. That was many years after Harlaw, where your two brothers died. The sack of Inverness and the bloody fight at Harlaw were the work, you will mind, of the same man, the King of the Isles, Donald MacDonald." He paused, his brow puckered in calculation. "Were he still alive, he would have been the grandfather of this Islesman, Donald Balloch. Neither you nor I have much to thank the MacDonalds for I am thinking, yet we are now with them although for a different reason in this feud against James Stewart the Accursed Whelp. We can no more seek to leave them now, than we could spit in their eyes last night, and hope to live. These Highlanders and Islesmen dinna think like you. I have heard you speak of chivalry. These folk have loyalty – fierce and possessive. They say, as the Vikings said seven hundred years since, 'Who is not for me, is against me.'" Kenneth Fraser stopped. Alastair looked at him with some resentment and much surprise. He finished fastening his boots.

"Very well my Highland friend. I accept you should know the Gael better than I. If we are to keep the friendship of these folk and not their lasting enmity, you are telling me we must finish this thing together. We may need the help of the Clan Donald before this feud is ended, so that your argument rings true."

"Ach weel," said Kenneth. "What are seven days lost. Even if you are right aboot Dunstaffnage and the Royal personages, could the twa of us mak much o' a difference?"

Out from Glencoe rode forty men. Donald Balloch, his feet almost sweeping the ground, was at the head of the Islemen. The Badger, Ian MacDonald of Glencoe, with Alastair Hogeston of Plewlands and Kenneth Fraser son of the smith of Invermoriston, took seventeen fighting men in his tail. The Ben Alder expedition lasted four days and three nights and it was as Alastair Hogeston had surmised. Of James Stewart there was no sign. But seventeen of his men were caught in the great corrie. The Badger's men climbed from Loch Ericht to the hidden valley by night, guided by Sam, Hogeston and Fraser and as dawn blanched the sky they scrambled down the steep slope, divided into two parties and swept the glen on either side of the loch. The bothies of the Stewarts crouched on the west shore and MacDonald's horsemen were in amongst them before they could rise from their straw. Broadswords made quick work of the sleepers. Ten who were alert jumped on their horses and of these, eight made their escape and rode for the mouth of the glen. Donald Balloch sat on a knoll with a clear view towards the loch and waited for them. Eight of his men rode to meet the fleeing Stewarts. Surprise was again total. The battle was swift and complete. Of James Stewart of Garth there was no sign and in the hour of dawn every Stewart was slaughtered with one exception. At the Badger's command the youngest, it seem, was spared. The MacDonalds with triumphant yells plundered the bothies then fired them. The Stewart horses were rounded up. The Stewart dead had their heads hacked off and their corpses were left to feed the buzzards, the foxes and the carrion crows.

By noon the raiders were ready to return to Glencoe. Not a MacDonald was lost. The captive Stewart was paraded before his conquerors and carefully, patiently, the reasons for the raid were explained to him, both the ambush at the Bridge of Awe and the rape of the MacDonald women in the Glen of Dierdre. The names of the victors were repeated until they were fully remembered. Then the survivor of the massacre was given a bag of meal and set on a strong horse.

"Now," roared the Badger. "Carry the tale of the events of this day to your master James Stewart of Garth. Tell him when next he plunders cattle and rapes women it had better not be Glencoe cattle or MacDonald women."

Thirteen

A strong west wind blew autumn into Glencoe. Squalls which swept in from the ocean fell in soft rain on the high corries. The sun was hidden by Bidean nam Bian, giant of the mountains but bright shafts of light sliced through storm-clouds, sparkled the slim white beards of the torrents and transformed green of bog moss to glowing emerald. The three ships were storm-bound in the loch. Their crews kept constant watch for a dragging anchor, their victuallers argued and bargained for salt meat, cheeses and hides, and wind plucked at the hair of sixteen grisly heads nailed to the masts.

The Badger with his distinguished ally celebrated their assault on the Ben Alder hideout. Hogeston and Fraser made their farewells and rode east up the wide valley then through the gorge of Glencoe to the Glen Etive track and so to the croft on the meadow of Dierdre. Aeneas MacDonald's face was full of woe. Six nights before, James Stewart had returned. He had two men with him and at the sight of them, Eilidh locked herself in her little room and screamed that she would cut her wrists if they broke in on her. Stewart laughed at her terror but bade his men leave her alone. He swept the struggling Morag into his arms and carried her to the bedroom where he had used her before. Next morning when they rode south Stewart left some pieces of money. "A Stewart takes what he wants but likes to ken the value of his chattels," he said to Aeneas, and with a broad wink to Morag, "I'll be back."

To the riders it seemed that MacDonald's threat to "kill the adder" held less anguish and menace than when he had screamed it to the mountains ten days before. Hogeston described the clan raid on Ben Alder.

"God bless you sirs," cried Aeneas. "You have revenged my poor daughters."

They were tightening the girths when a young woman came up Glen Etive weighted down with a load of firewood. She dropped her burden at the door, straightened her back, looked at her father and then at the strangers. Her hair was the shade of new shelled chestnuts and small pieces of bark and lichen were caught up in its long strands. Kenneth admired the stocky body, hips nipped in at the waist by a band of tow, and, under the tight spread of her dress, the plump swellings of her breasts. A woven plaid sheathed her from shoulders to knees in the colour of August heather. She stood like a doe, motionless, sensing for danger. Her right hand rested on the hilt of a long dagger and large eyes searched the faces of the strangers.

"These are the men I told you about, Morag lass," said her father softly. "They seek Stewart on a matter of revenge for murder. This is the law-man from Edinburgh, Alastair Hogeston, and this is Kenneth Fraser. Gentlemen, my daughter Morag."

"Gin I were a man, I would not be wasting my time at the croft of Dierdre." Her voice was low, her tone flat and cold. "Gin I were a man, James Stewart of Garth would be feed for the hoodie crows." She looked at her father and her young face grew hard. "Gin I were a man," she repeated.

Aeneas shifted his feet. "Now Morag," he said.

"Don't 'Now Morag' me father," she interrupted. "You will say you have had no chance to deal with James Stewart. You men must aye count numbers, and your chances. When the Beast comes here again," her young face was flushed, "Here he will bide, under the ground." Her eyes flew to Hogeston and Fraser. "Not because of what he has done to me – aye," she nodded towards Aeneas, "I can tell that he has told you. God help me I could have made Stewart rue the time he set eyes on me.

But for Eilidh's sake, the poor demented quine, he'll not again rise sated from my bed."

She turned abruptly through the door and out of sight. "Ach, she has a temper that one," said Aeneas with a shrug of resignation.

"Aye," said Kenneth staring thoughtfully after her. "And Christ help the Stewart should he stop here again."

They mounted and in a matter of minutes the croft on the meadow of Dierdre had disappeared behind the brown shoulder of the mountain.

Fourteen

Although he regretted deeply that James Stewart had not been included in the Ben Alder massacre, the knowledge that he had been correct in his estimation of Stewart's movements comforted Alastair. They were now ten days behind their enemy. The direction of the route confirmed the supposition that he was headed for Garth. It sprang to his mind that Stewart might be returning to witness or assist in the abduction of the young King and his mother from Dunstaffnage Castle. Livingston's purpose in encouraging the ambush of a Queen's messenger was now crystal clear to him. His father had been the innocent, sent callously to his death, and alive, he threatened Livingston's plan by exposing its deceit. How much of this was known or suspected by the household within the massive walls of Dunstaffnage? He remembered the Knight of Lorn's refusal to believe that Livingston was capable of such treachery. Alastair hoped that his father had recognised it and had sounded the warning, but it was only his poor pale ghost he had seen lying in the tower room. He dug his heels hard against his horse's flanks. "Kenneth, keep at the trot, we must reach Dunstaffnage quickly."

Darkness overtook them at the Bridge of Awe and once more that place cast its horrid premonition. The ground was heavily trampled. "What do you make of it Kenneth?" asked Hogeston. Fraser dismounted and studied the marks. "They have gone east, perhaps fifty horse."

"So we are too late again," said Alastair. Livingston has made his coup."

Across a small inlet of the sea the bulk of the castle loomed, faintly visible against the western glim. Its drawbridge was down, its portcullis up and Hogeston and Fraser rode straight into the heart of the fortress unchallenged.

"Guard," yelled Alastair. "Guard assemble."

There was a padding of feet, a clatter of arms, and a man appeared bearing a spluttering torch. He held it up at the horsemen.

"All right, you can enter."

"So, we can enter, can we? And what if our swords were unsheathed, could you stop us then? Where are your men? Why is the castle wide open? Where is your master?"

"So many questions," grumbled the master-at-arms. "My master left with Queen Joan and the young King ten hours since."

"Why? Who did they go with? Come man answer me properly," commanded Alastair.

"Why, Why, Why, you have me fair flummoxed," replied the soldier. "They rode off with the Regent Livingston. He demanded entrance. How was I to know not to admit the Regent? He carried the Royal Standard. I must have done wrong, for my master cursed me as he left. It wasn't my fault. I am only a soldier. Should I have known the Regent was unwelcome?"

Hogeston and Fraser dismounted. The man, still grumbling, led their horses to the stables.

"My God Kenneth," said Hogeston, "It has all happened as I feared it would. I should have shouted my suspicions when I was here. Damn Lorn with his outdated loyalties and his misguided chivalry. I thought my father would have told him-or did he never guess?" Fear stilled his voice. He turned abruptly and raced up the winding stair to the tower room where he had last seen Sir Philip Hogeston. A little old woman met him at the door. "Sir, Sir," she cried pushing against him. "You can't come in yet. He is not ready."

Alastair thrust her aside and entered the room. The smell of death took him by the throat. A candle guttered on a small wall-shelf and below it lay his father, the waxy pallor of dead skin already smoothing his features. Yellow bandages, stiff with putrescence hung from the stump of his right arm and a pool of blood clotted on the floor. His neck was stretched taut by the cloth sling which tied his lower jaw to the top of his head and a copper coin rested on each lid closing his eyes in the black stare of sightless death. His body was unnaturally twisted on its litter. The woman had been interrupted in her task of plugging the anus with a white pebble and Alastair felt his stomach heave.

"You shouldn't have come in," whined the hag. "When you see him tomorrow he will be different. They came and tore his bandages from his arm. He bled to death and, the black fiend take him, his murderer stood and laughed."

He threw open the shutter on the small window and breathed the cold sea air.

"Get on with your work," he said at last. "As you say I shall see him tomorrow. There is no hurry now."

Down the stair in the living quarters he found the castle's steward. Like the others he was dejected and ashamed.

"Livingston came upon the castle at the last light of day," he said. "He had a troop of fifty strong and demanded entrance in the name of the protector of Scotland. He bamboozled the captain of the guard into opening the gate, lowering the draw-bridge and allowing the armed men into the castle."

After that, thought Alastair, there was nothing anyone could do. The Black Knight, Queen Joan, with the young King, had their equipage transferred to the Regent's force and, with as much dignity as they could muster, rode off with Livingston that very morning. It was a bold coup, a bluff that had worked because the garrison was quite unprepared for this sort of attack. Livingston must have been surprised and delighted that he had captured the King, Queen Joan and her husband without a blow. He now had the power he needed and his rival, Crichton, could only twiddle his thumbs in Edinburgh Castle – and take orders!

Philip Hogeston, Knight of Plewlands, Duffus, in the Earldom of Moray, was buried at Dunstaffnage Castle on the third day of August, 1439.

Confidant and friend of King James the First of Scotland and of his Queen, crusader, erstwhile prisoner and priest of the Wolf of Badenoch at the castle in Lochindorb, he died of wounds inflicted at the Bridge of Awe in combat with his sworn enemy James Stewart, third son of the Wolf.

His body was returned to the bosom of mother earth on a bright summer morning in the small chapel graveyard to the seaward of the fortress gate. A brisk wind drifted spray from an ocean of racing white horses, and, when his body was lowered into the shallow hole, a flight of greenshank piped a careless requiem as they flashed across the isthmus to the pebbled beach out of the wind's tooth. Alastair, third son of the dead man stood by the grave on that rocky place and allowed the wind of sorrow to sweep over him. He heard again the peep peep of oyster-catchers on the beaches of the Moray Firth, the arrogant laugh of the herring gulls, and saw the little kittiwakes kiss each other on their ledges on the Covesea cliffs. He relived the terror and excitement of great heights as he swung at a rope's end and reached for eggs in inaccessible places. He heard again his father's voice above him, "Good lad. Push with your feet. I've got you safe." He remembered Peter Grant, his father's squire, and the tales he had told to his sisters and to himself at the end of their riding lessons. While the horses nuzzled into their feed bags, Peter talked of another horse, Dogulu, so swift and so clever, which had carried his father to victory over a French nobleman at a tournament at Dreux. Peter made every movement of Dogulu come alive for them and, like the ending in a fairy story, his father had won the hand of the Lady Bridget, their mother. He thought then of her and saw in the eye of his mind the sag of her body in the ravage of grief when she heard from him of her husband's death. It mattered now that he had grown apart from his father these last years. He had blamed him for this – his continual pre-occupation with the state of the Nation, his frequent absences from home, and his apparent lack of interest in the future of his only surviving son. Since his brothers had died on the blood soaked hill of the Harlaw, conceived though he was in the aftermath of that sorrow, Alastair was aware that part of his father too had died on that red field. He had come to realise that, even as a junior among the law makers of the realm, he knew more of the subtleties of intrigue and deceit that surrounded the Royal family than did Sir Philip.

Now, in the cold clasp of sorrow, he blamed himself for failing to give his father the honour that was his due and the love he constantly felt yet seldom showed. He was glad he had moved so swiftly to his father's bidding on this occasion but knew what Sir Phillip must have thought of him when he failed to appear on the day he was expected. Who knows but that his father, in his annoyance, may have advanced his departure from Stirling because of this. Often enough in the past Alastair had deliberately flaunted his unpunctual ways – and his father had known it.

Kenneth Fraser spoke beside him. "Tears winna bring back the dead. Come, there are things tae dae."

Fifteen

Hogeston and Fraser rode hard for Perth. They sheltered and rested their horses in the black houses of the hill folk, bedding down with sheep on their hay and their dung and in the company of hens roosting in the rafters. They went by Glen Lochy and Glen Dochart to Strath Earn and on the evening of the third day they approached Megginch Castle from the river Tay.

Lady Jean Hay, Alastair's sister and junior by two years was the one person who had been and was still closest to him. She was the last child of Bridget de Dreux and Philip Hogeston. From her French mother she inherited her vivacity and her slim athletic figure. Philip Hogeston had given her his dark complexion and strong cheekbones but she had her mother's mischievous blue eyes. Her nature was a blend of the Gallic and the Pictish characteristics of northeast Scotland. She was the most talented of the family, the wisest, thanks to French commonsense and she possessed the passionate love and the determination of her Scottish ancestors. When she was sixteen, she had fallen under the spell of Graham Hay youngest son of an arrogant clan. She eloped with him but found her dramatic revolt less than satisfactory. Graham's father arranged the full panoply of wedlock in the Kirk of St. Machiar in Aberdeen and invited her family. The Plewlands contingent turned out in strength and filled the bride's seats. Jean felt at first the tears of sudden rage and humiliation. Being three months with child she had not wished the ceremonial of marriage and now she was trapped by the establishment she pretended to despise. But because she was Jean, pride followed the tears as she counted the friendly, loved faces and at last her irrepressible sense of humour triumphed. By the time she knelt to take her vows she was shaken by giggles which Graham overcame only by squeezing her tightly and kissing her hotly on the mouth.

Now she stood in front of Alastair, eyes shining, lips already framing a spate of welcome.

"Alastair my darling, my love," she cried and threw herself at him. "Och you are wet and filthy foul as ever you were." Her dancing eyes met her brother's.

"The oak and the ash and the bonnie rowan tree," she sang, grabbing his arms, and the pair, children once more, pranced round the hall.

"Are all growing green in oor ain countree."

"This is my man, Kenneth Fraser," said Alastair. "You remember him?"

"Good day to you Kenneth," smiled Jean. "You can take yourself off to the kitchen. You look as hungry as a pair of curs. Alastair, when did you feed that ugly face of yours? And God! You do smell! Have you washed since I was last in Edinburgh? Come up to my room and you shall lie in Cleopatra's arms." Alastair looked in surprise at his sister.

"Cleopatra? Who is she?"

Jean giggled. "Cleopatra is my new French bath, so voluptuous and so naughty. She is made of burnished copper, shaped like a woman with her legs wide open and holds enough water to float a raft! Hot water and a good scrub will perhaps wash away the stink. Where have you been? You look as if you had crawled through a muck-midden.

"Right first time," laughed Alastair.

They had reached her room. She pulled him through the door and pushed him into a cushioned chair.

"Come now, off with your boots and your clothes and Cleopatra will be ready by the time you are. Maisie," she called. A girl no older than fourteen came running in.

"Maisie," said Jean, "meet my brother Alastair – my favourite brother which is nice for him being also my only brother. He is a fine looking man under all that dirt and still unmarried last time I saw him though heaven kens how many lassies have swooned for him." She addressed Alastair. "I tell Maisie to keep looking for the handsome one and lose no time in making him marry when she thinks she can do no better."

"Just what you did yourself Jean," said Alastair.

"Exactly," retorted his sister, "and I have been happy ever since and proud of my wee David, premature though he was." She turned to the girl. "Don't stand there gowking Maisie. Get the bath filled and tell Meg and Janet to help you. Isn't she lovely, Alastair – not Maisie you idiot, though you could do a lot worse – Cleopatra. Isn't she dissolute! Graham took her home to me from Paris. He is on the ambassador's staff and travels often. Doesn't she look deliciously vulgar! I want to see you wallow in her embrace." All this time she tugged and pulled at the laces on Alastair's riding boots and as she hauled them off the three girls poured buckets of steaming water into the copper bath.

"Now off with your claes and in as God made you," ordered Jean. She sprinkled a handful of crushed dried petals in the water. "There are some Arabian roses to sweeten the odours."

She caught hold of her brother's shirt and pulled it over his head. "Come on girls, help the poor man to his nuptials with Cleopatra."

Alastair, head covered by his shirt heard the squeals and giggles as three pairs of hands busied themselves on his breeks and when they were off he was pushed and led to the bath.

"Don't scald me now. Hot water takes my skin off."

"It is lovely my pet," said Jean. "It wouldn't burn a baby's bum."

The girls giggled as Alastair stepped gingerly into the tub.

"Eh, what a well made man he is! Don't fret," said Jean to the bashful male. "They have all seen at least one before and comparison is part of the fun of being a woman."

"Honestly, Jean," said Alastair, "You don't improve. You always were a bawd and marriage to Graham Hay hasn't helped."

"You ought to be grateful Graham took a fancy to me," replied his sister. "At least he made an honest woman of me and spared me father's rages and mother's blushes. God! What fun we used to have. I am glad you still have Kenneth Fraser. I used to love that tow-haired rascal. I remember when I rolled him off the cliff at Covesea! The randy lad was getting a bit too close and much too serious. I don't know yet how I got out from under him but over the edge he went and made a beautiful splash. It was lucky the tide was in! The look on his face as he hit the sea was so comical I laugh whenever I think of it!"

That night Alastair and Jean ate on their own. Graham Hay was in Aberdeen. Jean said his father suffered from dropsy and had asked his youngest son to come and amuse him. Graham was his Benjamin and his best loved and had the knack, given to youngest sons, of treating his father as an equal. He had an inexhaustible fund of bawdy stories and his father enjoyed his company, feeling his years fall off him when he was about. Jean missed her man but was proud that of all his family he was the most asked for by her father-in-law.

"Are you not surprised to see me Jean?" asked Alastair. "No," she replied. "I think I know why you are here. It is father is it not? He told me a bit about the reason for his journey to Dunstaffnage and I have been studying your face. Ever since it was washed clean of dirt it has been plain to read. Something terrible has happened. Is he dead?"

"Aye, he is," said Alastair quietly. The room became still. Jean sat bold upright, her long dark hair framing her face, her blue eyes the colour of shadowed snow.

"Well," she said at last, "Go on." Alastair told her the facts from his wakening in Edinburgh to the sound of the sailor's knocking until the windy afternoon at Dunstaffnage Castle when he had buried his father in the small graveyard overlooking the Firth of Lorn. There was a long silence and Alastair knew without looking that his sister, Jean, the boisterous, laughing Jean, was weeping. He sat and waited. Jean's shoulders stopped shaking and she dried her tears. She looked at him through red eyes.

"What are we going to do about it, you and I?"

"That's my Jean," he said.

"I have been to Castle Garth," she continued as if he had not spoken. "It's a brute of a place, like its lord. James Stewart is the only man who has ever sent a shiver down my spine. The shiver of wanting I know well enough but this other feeling, only once. He undresses his women with his eyes and there is something else there when he looks at you. Perhaps the herring see it in the eyes of the gannet or the frightened rabbit in the eyes of the stoat. He has, I have heard, the performance of a stallion, the appetite of Hercules, and the habits of a cur. Graham took me to Garth last summer to engage a gardener, a man reputed to be a magician with fruit trees. I knew who I was meeting, but James Stewart did not. Mother told me about the sons of the Wolf of Badenoch and of Mariota de Athyn's warning to father especially to beware of James her third son. But I had no reason to think the feud still smouldered. God, I know better now. Father, I honestly think, had forgotten about it. He spent a night with Graham and me before going to Stirling to see that rat Livingston, a man more fit to govern Hell than Scotland. He talked about the old days and I chaffed him about his secret passions – he was in love with the Wolf's Mariota before he met mother you know – and I asked him if he had killed any fierce wolves recently. James Stewart calls himself The Fierce Wolf."

She stopped suddenly, her bright eyes on Alastair's face. "Didn't you know about father's love affair with Mariota de Athyn?" She laughed, "Mon Dieu, how simple you men are! Story has it that she was banished from Lochindorb for witchcraft. It is much more likely that she was removed for unfaithfulness. Father escaped, but the curse of James Stewart dogged him always. I asked Peter Grant to tell me about that curse. He said that even in the kitchens of Lochindorb Castle they heard James' scream. James had always hated father – he probably knew what was going on and brooded on his knowledge as a teenager would." Alastair remembered his own wet youthful dreams of a woman called Mariota. He said quickly, "When you met him a year ago did he look the kind of man who could keep hate a-flame for forty years?"

"You have made it hard for me to answer. What I must do is to sweep from my memory all you have just told me of father's murder and see James Stewart as if that had not happened." She sat silent for a little time. "I saw indulgence, perversion, and cruelty in that face. Yes the man I saw at Garth could have had hate festering in his gut."

Jean's face became still and a questioning look appeared in her eyes. "But though he exposes to the world the profile of the Fierce Wolf, behind the mask something else lurks, something perhaps only a woman sees."

"By those that hate him he is also known in the Gaelic tongue as Chuilein Churta," said Alastair, "The Accursed Whelp!"

Jean thought for a moment. "It is something to do with his vanity," she mused. "The chink in his armour may be his overbearing arrogance, his blind self assurance, especially in his attitude to women." Her eyes looked full at Alastair and he had a quick glimpse of the powerful intuitive searching mind of his sister.

"So," he mused, "you think that James Stewart The Fierce Wolf of Garth has the heel of Achilles?" He paused. "Why is he called 'The Fierce Wolf'? Heaven knows his father the Wolf of Badenoch was wild enough."

"It could be meant as a deliberate sneer at his father," said Jean. "A man like James would never sympathise with weakness, and he would not understand why his father, the King's brother, should choose to beg forgiveness of the church and accept public humiliation as his penance."

Alastair Hogeston thought about this for a moment. "Guid kens the name fits," he said. "What I saw at the Bridge of Awe leaves me in no doubt. Tell me about your meeting with him at Garth."

"On our way Graham and I stopped for a while in Aberfeldy. You know how quick an ear Graham has for a new song. There was a piper in the village that day, a McIver. He was tipsy but man, could he bla'! The landlord had served us a fine meal. I remember it because it was so tasty – roasted squirrels with walnut and oatmeal stuffing."

Alastair laughed. "Why you are not built like a sow I will never understand," he said. "You always ate the most – and cleaned up for the rest of us."

"There are other things I like as much as good food but they are not so easy to come by," said Jean. "Just as we were served this dainty dish the piper fellow started on a pibroch outside – a gloomy tune full of grace notes and trills. Graham went to the door and shouted at him, 'Are all your clan dead that you can play nothing but a funeral dirge?' The McIver looked as if he would draw his dirk but Graham softened the insult by saying he had heard of the courage of the McIvers of Glen Lyon and could he play a rousing battle song or did he not dare, so near to Garth? The McIver struck the bait like a pike and swore he would pipe his clan to Hell and back in pursuit of the one who called himself The Fierce Wolf, that whelp, that upstart fellow in Garth Castle who could not stop his fornicating long enough to unsheathe his sword instead of his cock. Graham said he would pay for his dinner if he could make a song out of that. The man had great spirit and he blew a ranting jolly tune that fair set the feet dancing and the hills ringing."

Alastair laughed. Then his face became thoughtful. "Do you think that there is bad blood between the Clan McIver and James Stewart of Garth? MacDonald of Glencoe suggested there was and now you say that Graham has knowledge of it and that the piper confirms it."

"Och Alastair," chided Jean. "Forget you are a law man and let me tell my story in my own time. You are always in such a hurry to get to the nub but if you listen you will learn it all. I dare say the clan McIver is a bit fearful for its cattle with that predatory wolf's whelp down the Glen. Our business in Castle Garth – or rather Graham's business – was with the steward, John Menzies, so it was for him that Graham asked. Menzies showed me to one of the top rooms, a bonnie place overlooking the Strath of Appin and the river Tay. He sent his wife Kirsty to entertain us. He must also have told his master about me for scarcely had Kirsty and I started on the gossip when in strode himself, James Stewart of Garth. He had been drinking, his face was flushed and his tongue a wee bit big for his mouth but very correct.

"He doffs his cap to me, drops a bow as neat as a dancing master and said, 'You have the prettiest hair Mistress Hay I have seen this side of London.' Well my hair was all mussed up by the journey and that just wasn't true. I brindled a bit and retorted. 'And you are the prettiest liar I have met this side of Paris.' He threw his head back and laughed. 'My God, Mistress Hay, and that makes me some liar, for the French lie to conceal their absurdities which are many. When, if ever, did you visit Paris Mistress Hay?' He didn't know that I had a French mother and considered myself as French as I was Scottish but I was not going to let him off with that impudent remark. In my best French I threw back at him, 'Some Scotsmen are born absurd and can't conceal it however hard they lie.'"

"You ought to have seen Kirsty's face. Fingers to her mouth she gaped at me and waited for James Stewart's rage to burst. Instead, he stood like a stag in rut, still and wary, tense and magnificent in his fine leathers. We glared at each other each testing the strength of the other's gaze. I am good at that as you know Alastair and, after a while, he lifted a hand in mock salute and replied in French, 'I salute you Mistress Hay for your fearless repartee. Kirsty, look after our guest as she were your own mistress for I doubt not we shall both see more of her in days ahead.' Then he bowed again long and slow, his eyes never leaving mine and left the room as swiftly as he had entered."

"Jean," interrupted Alastair, "I know you are a great one with the men but you will speak too boldly once too often. You haven't described James Stewart to me yet."

"Man, if you dinna ken him noo it's no fault of mine. What else di ye want to know? He is a long whip of a man, thin as an ash. He pads his shoulders to give him greater width I am sure. He has a fine face, a well singed beard, blue black hair with an odd steak of white in it and big eyes like a stallion's, under white brows."

"Tell me about the steward, John Menzies."

"He is a hard man to bargain with. Tom Torrance was indentured to Castle Garth as apprentice gardener and Graham had to pay Menzies well for his release. But we have a rare gardener in Tom and well worth the money."

"Has Menzies been steward to James Stewart for long?" asked Alastair.

"Yes. I heard Graham say his father had been bee-keeper at Lochindorb to the Wolf of Badenoch, so that John Menzies was in their service since he was born. By his name, I expect he came from Weem when the Wolf of Badenoch betrothed James as an infant to Janet Menzies. It was then that the Wolf secured the lands of Garth and built his eyrie for his own wild purposes. Garth is a fortress as you shall see and not a couthie place to bide in, which may, in part, explain its owner's pleasure in fire and rape. What else can you expect of a wolf's whelp in a lair like Castle Garth?"

"Have you seen anything of James Stewart since then?"

"I have not," said Jean. "But twice he had been in Perth and sent a man to me with a letter written and signed by himself. Ach, he hasn't much imagination. They each bore the same message." She paused, eyes twinkling waiting for Alastair's question.

He laughed. "Well Jean, and what was James Stewart saying that was so important he had to say it twice?"

"Of no importance at all. The man's a rogue and knows all the tricks. The message, fastened mark you by the Stewart seal, said crudely:

'Gardeners are bought

Good woman are not.

A husband shall rot

Ere love can be sought?'

"A hope or a promise?" asked Alastair curtly.

"Neither," said Jean. "Bloody arrogance."

Sixteen

"Jean," said Alastair next morning, "I am going to take a look at Garth. I can make no plans until I see the place and measure up its master."

"How do you intend to do that, my fine laddie?" said his sister. "Do you think you can climb the brae to the castle, knock on the yet and ask yourself to supper with James Stewart?"

"Will you listen to me you daft quine. James Stewart has never set eyes on me and if I cannot invent a good excuse to get inside his castle walls I might as well resign as a law adviser to the Court of King James and take up bee-keeping.

"You said it yourself," said Jean. "You'd have a better chance of getting into Castle Garth if you were a bee than a law man." She studied her brother's face. "You have far more of the French in you than I have. With your la de da voice and your aristocratic nose you are more like grandpere le Compt de Dreux than poor old dad. I have the Hogeston stamp I suppose but I don't recollect boasting of my origins in front of James Stewart of Garth. And I have an open invitation to visit him. Join me as my escort and you are in."

Alastair looked at his sister. "Graham would never allow it and I will not let you run such a risk."

"Forget about Graham. He will be in the bosom of his family for a further two weeks and a trip with you to Strath Tay will suit me very well. I shall take Maisie and you can have Kenneth Fraser. I will send word to Stewart that we are coming and the castle will be ours for as long as we want to stay."

"You are sure he doesn't know you are a Hogeston?" asked Alastair.

"Would he be writing poems to me if he knew I was daughter of the adulterous priest?" She laughed. "Dinna worry Alastair, I am looking forward to our journey. First, we must warn mother that you are delayed. You say you sent her a message from Glencoe. She will not know then that father is dead, and she must not learn from rumour."

"I shall hate to break the news to her," said Alastair.

"My bonnie man, only you can grasp that thistle. You are the only one who can tell her all she will want to know. She will ask about everything, even the colour of the last stone dropped on his grave. "Struth! The day father came home after yon trip of his to Edinburgh when he caught you leching wi' the two quines when you should have been meeting him at Leith, mother made him describe every single thing he could remember, about your room, about the girls in the bed, if they were cheeky or afraid, pretty or pert. Of course she had to know about you too, what you said, what you were wearing – which was easy answered! God! When I got the picture I took such a fit of the giggles! I wasn't supposed to be listening or even to be in the room at the time so I should have had my bottom skelped. But mother was trying hard just then to suppress her own smiles so all I got was a rough 'to your room girl' from father."

Following the well worn track up the river Tay, Jean and Alastair rode to Aberfeldy. On the journey they discussed Alastair's role. Jean was all for disguising him as her steward and had invented a plausible enough excuse for a visit to Castle Garth. Alastair was looking farther ahead.

"You know what will happen if we enter under any subterfuge and are recognised?" he asked her. "I certainly will never see daylight again and I don't relish spending the rest of my life in Castle Garth's dungeon. Your fate could be even worse. If we continue this dangerous exercise, Jean, we must conceal as little as possible. By all means let us pretend you are seeking to sell some of your fishing rights on the Tay but I shall present myself as a legal relation of yours protecting your interest and enjoying the outing. I used to be known as Oggie so I can be called Alastair Og."

The river rippled in August sunlight and its still pools mirrored the different greens of ash, birch, yew and pine.

"Do you remember the woods near Evreux, Nick?" She used his

childhood name. "Do you remember that marvellous year when we became French at the Chateau de Dreux? And the crush Catherine had on the pompous Monsieur Bray? Do you remember dancing in the streets of Evreux after the battle of Baugé, the bittersweet of victory not knowing then if father was alive or dead. What fun we had when we returned; the picnics in the field by the stream and mother looking so young and so much in love. Di ye mind when you had to hide from old 'Dootie' after she caught you fishing for her hens with worms on fish-hooks! And the excitement," continued Jean, "when the English besieged Dreux. Were you afraid? I was. Did you think we were in such terrible danger?"

"Of course not," lied Alastair. "I was thirteen and pulling my long-bow with the rest. You were eleven Jean and only a girl. What could you have known of war?"

"I knew enough," Jean replied. "I remember helping mother in the laundry sorting out old linen to bind the soldiers' wounds. There was only one great captain in the Scottish army when they scattered the English outside the gates of Dreux – not John Stewart of Darnley and Evreux – but father. I remember being lifted up on to his horse as he crossed the draw-bridge and gripping his mailed wrist with one hand and the horse's mane with the other. I remember the smell of sweat and oil and the slimy feel of blood. His right glove was dark red and sticky. Oh! He was my hero then and always." Her voice, high with excitement, suddenly dropped. "That is why we must plot and plan our revenge. Nicky, we must not let him down."

The tavern in Aberfeldy lay close to the bridge of Tay. It was a substantial building converted to a hostelry by its present owner from a ruined bridge-fort. The man remembered Jean – what man would not – and Alastair was introduced as Alastair Og her brother.

"Have the McIvers shifted their tents," asked Jean, "or where is the bold piper today?"

"Mercy lady," said the innkeeper, "he is never far away. It's hard enough to get rid of the rascal so pray don't encourage him."

"Send him to me," said Jean imperiously.

The landlord returned looking less than pleased with the big McIver at his tail. When the piper saw Jean he broke into a shambling run, pushed the little man aside and advanced, both arms outstretched.

"Enough McIver," commanded Jean in Gaelic. "If I wanted a tulzie wi' you it wouldn't be here."

The man laughed and replied in the same tongue.

"What man wouldn't welcome a tulzie with you, lady, here or any place."

The wee landlord exploded in rage.

"Take your filthy suggestions and your filthy rags out of my hostelry," he spluttered.

"Let him be, landlord," said Jean. "I have something to say to this McIver – to himself alone," she ended significantly. Affronted, the small man left the room in even worse humour.

"Now McIver," said Jean, "I know you can speak the tongue of the Edinburgh folk and we will speak that tongue here in Aberfeldy because we will be understood by no more than a handful of folk and they are all in this room. I want you to take a message to your chief in Glen Lyon."

"Yes lady," said the piper in silken English. "I like you and I will take your story to the McIver."

"Tell him that two who hate the Stewart are seeking to enter Garth Castle. We shall get in but we cannot be sure of getting out. I think we shall be unharmed in the castle even if the Fierce Wolf finds out who we are. When we leave we may be followed and murdered. Ask the McIver to help us pass through Strath Tay."

"Aye lady," said the big fellow. "You take a risk indeed and I am sure it must be worth taking or you would not be here. I shall tell my chief and you can trust the McIvers to help the enemies of James Stewart."

"Now pipe us a tune my bonnie man – a defiance to James Stewart – like the last you blew for me." Jean laughed. "Wha kens, I may so occupy his thoughts, his cock may rise before his sword, as you said before in your song McIver."

Seventeen

They rode out from Aberfeldy next morning. It was a splendid day, clear and fresh after heavy rain. The river was in a brown flood that pulled at the pillars of the bridge. The green strath lay like a long snake between the mountains of Breadalbane black with pine forest and the dancing silver birches that clothed the slope of Weem Hill. They took the high path and in a short time looked down on the castle home of the Menzies. Woodpeckers hammered in the forest; families of crested tits flitted ahead of them through the firs picking at young cones and the track wound higher into the hills above the hamlet of Dull. To the south-west Ben Lawers pushed its massive bulk above the woods of Drummond Hill.

Alastair reined his horse and turned to Kenneth Fraser. "This is as far as you go with us Fraser. I cannot have anyone in Castle Garth who could become a hostage. It is likely that Lady Jean and I will be safe as long as we are within its walls. If the worst happens and we are unmasked even James Stewart will let us leave freely. He is of the Royal blood and, like all true noblemen, is bound by his code of chivalry. This afternoon or tomorrow morning we shall be on our way back to Aberfeldy. It is then that our lives may be in danger. The McIver will protect us as we leave, but I will be more at ease if you are where you can watch the approaches of the castle. Stewart may be preparing a surprise for us even now and I would like as much warning of mischief as I can get. If you scent danger light a fire on that hill over there and we shall know to cross the Tay by the swinging bridge below Dull."

"I would rather be with you master but if you think I will be of greater help on the outside then that is the way it must be," replied Fraser.

An hour before noon they left the hill path and rode down to the Keltney burn at Coshieville. Ragged bairns playing at the ford ran helter-skelter into a thatched bigging when they saw the horses, then crept out to gawk at the "lord and lady" riding by. The road to Garth rose steeply behind the hamlet and followed the tumbling burn for a mile. Woods on either side were felled and the brushwood burnt. No cover remained save in the gorge on the right. Alastair studied the fortifications as they approached. The castle, the simplest form of square tower built of rough cut stone soared unadorned to a parapet sixty feet above an iron gateway. It was stark and menacing and occupied the point of confluence of two rivers which roared through ravines of sheer red rock. The track crossed the westerly of the two gorges by a narrow wooden bridge then swung south to a man-made ditch which formed the base of the triangle of flat ground on which the Wolf of Badenoch had built his castle fifty years before. The ditch was spanned by another bridge and Alastair and his sister rode the last fifty yards to the castle closely watched by soldiers on the parapet. The gate was opened by an old man who cursed and swore as he pushed at the heavy doors. They dismounted in a small courtyard and their horses were led away to be stabled in the basement. A man-at-arms led them through a door on the left from where they ascended a long narrow stairway inside the wall. The stair climbed, turned and climbed again. Halfway up within the north wall a door opened inward and they entered the hall of Garth Castle. It occupied the entire width and breadth of the fortress and was lit by tall narrow windows, three on each of three walls. A fireplace with stone chimney seats occupied the east side of the hall and emblazoned above it on carved stone were the coats of arms of Badenoch, Buchan and Mar. From the domed ceiling clusters of crusie lamps hung low over a round oak table. Chairs were set against the walls between fixed stone benches and all were draped with rugs and hides. Two enormous bear-skins lay like grinning monsters on the hearth, brown pelts and claws spread-eagled on the floor.

John Gorm Stewart, son of James, introduced himself. He was a man in his thirties and Jean's height. His face was plump and smooth, unscarred by pox, untired by care. His eyes were sharp and bright like beech leaves in the spring. Alastair recalled how, at the command of the Estates, he had composed a letter of gratitude and commendation to this man. Here stood John Gorm Stewart, John of the blue armour who with Robert Reoch chief of the Clan Robertson and Black Colin of Glenorchy, had hunted and captured the murderers of King James I, Robert Graham and his accomplices Colquhoun and Chalmers. When he remembered how these men had died Alastair gave a sudden shudder. Their torture was ordered and planned by Queen Joan herself who watched, her face impassive as if carved from alabaster, hour upon dreadful hour while they were crushed, twisted, drawn, mutilated and blinded, inched to the brink of madness and beyond. It was her will that Death should overtake the killers of her beloved James at snail's pace. As a junior in the law department Alastair had been compelled to watch her horrific revenge to the final scream of her last victim.

John Gorm Stewart received them courteously and led them to an alcove by a window overlooking the Strath of Appin. A man who could only be his father sat in a high-backed chair. He was about twenty years older than his son and dressed in black velvet trimmed richly with ermine. His well singed beard was flecked with grey but his hair was strong and black. A lock of pure white swept like a coronet across the front of his brow. He had a long lined face and the eyes beneath white brows brooded like those of a lynx.

"Have ye lost your manners James Stewart or have I become an old bag in the twelvemonth since we met?" Jean's eyes flashed and she stamped her foot. Stewart's gaze did not leave her brother. His voice was silky soft.

"John Gorm, show the Lady Jean to her seat and bring her wine." He addressed the soldier by the door. "O'Halloran, fetch Magnusson." A young man entered and Stewart beckoned him forward until he stood an arm's length from Alastair.

"Alastair Og, have you seen this man before?" He spoke slowly, flicking his words at Hogeston. Alastair turned his head and looked at the boy. The trap was sprung. Before him stood the young prisoner whom the Badger and Donald Balloch had spared after the battle at Ben Alder and who had been well prompted to carry the news of the massacre to his master. Hogeston said nothing and turned again to face Stewart.

James Stewart watched him. "You are silent. So you are of the band which slaughtered my men in the corrie. You were recognised by this fellow as you approached the castle." He paused and Alastair saw his eyes waver for the first time as he searched to find the information he lacked, then he looked hard at Jean, studying her young face thoroughly and thoughtfully. He sighed and settled himself on the high oak chair. "So," he said and stroked his beard with his left hand. His eyes fixed again on Alastair. He was breathing slowly and deeply and a flush coloured the skin over his cheekbones. The room became deathly still. "Before you were born my father sat in this chair and condemned Philip Hogeston to the water pit in Lochindorb Castle." He paused. Outside, on pointed wings, swifts screamed. Far below the two rivers roared in their granite cage.

"I remember crouching at the top of the well and listening to his splashing in the darkness. I was fourteen years old and hated him even then." His voice, almost a whisper, stopped as past scenes became vivid in his memory. His long frame slumped in the chair.

"My father died in this castle, a wasted wreck of a man but feared as the very Devil." He was talking now of the Wolf of Badenoch, the Scourge of God, the Destroyer. "He built Garth for me when I was a child and for my wife Janet Menzies whose father gifted him the land as a dowry. We were babes when we were betrothed. It is plain now that he designed Garth as an outpost of his Highland kingdom and as a stranglehold on the lands of Tay. Janet and I have lived in this castle since we were wed but it became our home, if it ever has been a home, only after he died. He was here during the last foul and loathsome year

of his life. This castle was his tomb, the last lair of a stricken Wolf."
Stewart's voice stopped and silence swooped into the sun-flecked hall.
"I alone tended him in his final painful months. Janet would not bear
to look at him. Only his spirit blazed. His body died, or rotted, piece
by piece, poisoned years before by a treacherous woman, his wife my
mother and by her priest of Baal, your father."

Jean was wide-eyed, her face drained of colour. Alastair waited
straining to catch each syllable. "The Wolf had beaten them, Bishop
Bur, King Robert, all save Death and Philip Hogeston. Then, there
was only Philip Hogeston."

Stewart looked directly at Alastair. "I had forgotten about you." He
spoke lightly as if to himself. "You are the one who had been standing
on my shadow since the fight at the Bridge of Awe. You must have
whisked the cattle away from Ben Alder. My men told tales of water
kelpies and wild dogs and an avalanche like the crack of doom. And
you found and destroyed my nest of brigands in the great corrie.
Perhaps you hoped to destroy me too." Hate gleamed in his eyes. "I
am glad your father's end was slow. When I struck off his hand and
watched it, gripped to his sword, arch into the alders by the river Awe,
I knew what I would do to him; that he would long for death as had
my father The Wolf under the spell of his malignant priest. My
soldiers were quick. They finished off the Duffus troop on the bridge
and as they were being shot from horseback I fought and overcame
your father. To stop him dying I pulled his pulsing stump through the
bracelet he wore and stemmed the gush of his blood. Christ, when I
saw that band of gold with its entwined wildcats on his arm I could
have hacked his head from his treacherous body. That gold chain had
belonged to Mariota my mother, fashioned from the Bishop's treasure.
I spat on Hogeston's face. "Ere long you hog, these wildcats will drag
you into Hell.'" James Stewart's gaze was on Alastair but the mind
behind the eyes was at the Bridge of Awe and his moment of victory
on that trampled muddied road between the alders. He showed brown
teeth in a grin of triumph. "Later, when I tore the cloths from his arm

in that room at Dunstaffnage I pulled off this twisted armlet, this symbol of my mother's infidelity with your father. He bled to death."

He drew up his sleeve to show the bracelet of gold that twined round his arm. "I looked down on him as he lay beyond help in that small bright room, and as his life's blood poured out over the floor I cursed him again as I had cursed him forty years before. 'Die you adulterer, you poisoner, you warlock. Die at the hand of your sworn enemy, James Stewart of Garth.'"

Stewart paced in a slow circle round Hogeston. Suddenly he stopped. "Alastair Hogeston," he said, "it is now either me or you. O'Halloran, fetch wine, blood red wine. There is a toast I would have us drink."

Claret spilled into two golden goblets. Stewart raised his above his head. "To Death, Hogeston, to Merciless Death."

The two men stared at each other. There was a rustle of cloth and Jean stood between them.

"You mad fools," she cried and dashed the golden vessels from their hands. "You drink with Death as you were his equal! Alastair Hogeston, are you fey? And you James Stewart, do you think Death cares two hoots if you come to him bragging or begging? He kens weel you'll meet Him when He ca's the tune. Pick up these cups O'Halloran and fill them full. Drink ye silly men. Mak me the toast, or Lady Janet, or any braw quine wha takes your fancy, but dinna waste good wine on Death, that greedy strumpet." Words swarmed from Jean like wasps from a damaged byke. "James of Garth, would you choose to risk all this on the edge of my brother's sword?" She swept an arm in an arc that included the rich Persian carpets, the glowing tapestries and three windows that framed like paintings of a Florentine master the sparkling Tay and its flaming birches. She looked him square in the face. "You act like a child," she said, "A boy whose conduct has been sullied by childish hates and whose vision is blinded by the fancies of his fumbling youth. You have built your memory of my father from disputable wickedness and imagined wrongs. A poisoner, an adulterer, a warlock you say? Were Sir Philip Hogeston all or any of these things would he have dared return, unarmed to the Wolf's lair in Lochindorb? Should he have died so miserably by the sword of a mortal man? Would we be here now at your mercy in Garth? Na my fine mannie, lees canna drown the facts nor all your bluster and bombast mak me believe you had lawful cause to murder my father. You suffered you say as you watched the Wolf waste to shrivelled death. And revenge ye maun hae? Is there not a thocht in your heid James Stewart that whispers that the Wolf had mair to fear from Mariota his wife than from a young and misguided priest?"

Jean faced the lord of Garth. An arm's length away, her brother watched her in admiration. What was she trying to do? Was she prodding this man into a rash move? Did she hope to change Stewart's purpose? Was she just being Jean, fighting to her last breath? Sunset lit her hair and at her feet the women who had worked their shining rug in distant Turkestan blazed their approval in yellows and greens.

Jean waited. Would James Stewart strike her? She smelled his sharp male scent. She watched his eyes and knew the sudden shock of triumph. She had aimed well and hit the mark.

"Rage becomes you Mistress Jean." He turned and strode to his chair. "My mother," he said at last, "My mother was the most beautiful, the most passionate, and the most unprincipled woman I have ever known." His voice was low. "We all loved her, even Andrew who had more cause to fear and hate her." He paused. "Have you ever handled the new-born kits of a pine marten in their nest and then explored the hole in the tree a day later and felt your fingers touch nothing but blood and sticky hair? When he was thirteen, Andrew was ill, so ill he had the stink of death on him. No one was allowed into his room save my father and my mother, but we could hear his screams at night and the rasp of his breathing as we passed his door. My mother, Mariota, grew thin. Her face became sharp and brooding. Then we missed her for two nights and two days. Only our old nurse would creep to the boy's bedside with whey and gruel, for my father spent all day in the west tower where the figure of the naked Christ hung on the wall. He had slept there before but only when he was very drunk or angry. At night I could not sleep but lay afright listening to the padding of the Wolf's feet through the rooms and along the dark corridors of the castle. Then Mariota appeared again and it was as if nothing had happened.

"Andrew got better. Your father the priest carried him from that small room. He lit fires and boiled his witch's brew until the castle air was thick with steam, the smell of mint and the sound of his incantations. Weeks after he had recovered, Andrew made me swear to tell no living soul and told me that mother had tried to smother him. She had cried out, 'Child you are touched by the Evil One and possessed by demons. I must slay you lest they escape and harbour in my body.' The Wolf found her and dragged her screaming from the boy's room. Andrew recovered, but Philip Hogeston's foul influence was established in our castle. He had exorcised the devils from Andrew and succoured them in his own heart. All this he did so that he could destroy my father." He fingered the chain that twisted round his wrist, unfastened it and held it in the palm of his hand.

"The Wolf paid for this bauble with his right arm. His shoulder and neck were torn by an arrow in the raid on the Bishop's gold at the Bay of the Primroses. It was a lucky shot fired in the dark at the Lang Steps. The Devil's own luck for it was aimed and fired by Philip Hogeston. That was the beginning of it, the start of a long battle for my father's mind. Hogeston won. The Wolf lost his reason and grovelled at Bishop Bur's feet in the monastery of the Blackfriars at Perth. He went mad before he died."

With his free hand he loosened the tunic at his throat. His face was bathed in sweat. There was a tiny tinkle and the bracelet hung like a writhing snake from between his finger and thumb.

"This is the Devil's treasure." His voice was thick, his white brows drawn tight in anger.

"When my father robbed the Holy Church of its gold on the beach at the Bay of Primroses he robbed the Bishop of nothing but trouble. He met your father in the fight and he carried off the golden ornaments which later he melted down and recast into platters, drinking cups and – this." The gold serpent twisted slowly from his fingers.

"This was what he fashioned for Mariota." He flicked his wrist and the chain flew up and into his palm.

"A golden snake, as insidious as the Serpent of Eden, with the heads of two wildcats." He held the thing out for Jean and Alastair to examine. There they were, the gleaming heads, jaws agape, ears pricked back against their skulls and two pairs of green eyes glowing hate.

"When she danced – which was often for she delighted in her body and in the movement of her limbs – when she danced, that golden gliding reptile caught the attention of men, with its emerald cats' eyes flashing low on her belly. I watched her and I watched them, their gaze glued to her long thighs and her undulating hips and I would see the wet tongues move over their lips. Oh, she made all men her slaves. The Wolf knew it and encouraged her, but I have seen him take swift revenge on those so rash as to grasp at the serpent. And yet, for all his cunning, he failed to see where danger lusted, clothed in the robe of his captive priest." He sat brooding, his eyes on Jean. He rose abruptly and said in a tone suddenly light and almost merry, "You will sup with me. Lady Jean, your arm. Hogeston, will you honour me at my table."

The table was laid and the meal was served in the smaller dining chamber above the hall. Janet Stewart was already supervising the tasting when her husband entered, Jean on his arm and she gave him a shrewd glance. She looked older than her years, a little portly woman with a lined face that mirrored the sadness of her life. The ladies curtseyed and were soon in conversation, about Tom Torrance the gardener, the fashions of the court, the freedom that children expected and the liberty they took with their elders, and later, about men and the difficulties that women made for themselves. "I have reached the stage," said Janet Stewart, "where I leave my man to his own devices. It wisna always so, but now, if my husband disnae come hame in complete disorder or smelling of the whorehouses, I accept him to my bed without the inquisition he would have had lang syne. But it's nae often noo he shares my bed," she added wistfully.

John Gorm, and especially his French wife Marie, made themselves pleasant to the strangers. Marie was impatient to hear the gossip of the capital. She was quick to emphasise her kinship with the Duke of Burgundy and was adept at name-dropping. Despite himself, Alastair found that he was feeding her with the tit-bits of court scandal she longed to hear.

"Hark at the auld fish-wife I have for a brother," joked Jean.

Other than to address some trite remark to Jean, the Lord of Garth said nothing. He sat aloof at the table head, his smouldering gaze now on Jean, now on Hogeston. It was as if having opened a window on the cellar of his soul he had pulled it shut again.

They left Garth in the late afternoon. Although the murder-hole lay await somewhere on the long stair, Jean and her brother left unharmed. But when they reached Dull a bonfire danced on the hill above. Fraser had seen something that aroused his suspicion and they rode quickly to the swing-bridge, glad to have the McIvers with them. Kenneth Fraser met them at the river and urged them to take a route by Bolfrack's Hill to the Urlar burn.

"McIver is sure a trap will be set for you and you must gain the safety of Loch na Creige by night."

"Tell the McIver I shall be back and will hope to enlist his help again."

"Tell him yourself," grinned Kenneth and he added, "I will keep Maisie safe and amused and return her to Megginch." He doffed his cap in an exaggerated salute to Jean and rode off.

Eighteen

They picked their way into the mountains and reached the pass and the loch as it was growing dark. A man rose out of the heather and said in good English "Alastair Hogeston and Lady Jean Hay, the McIver is pleased to receive you." He grasped Jean's bridle and led them up a small glen towards a low flat-topped hill. "You will leave your horses here." Two men came from the dusk and took charge of the animals. Their guide picked up a piece of rock and struck the heather four times in rhythmic hollow thuds. Far away in the twilight a stag roared. The man knocked on the mound again and a hole opened in the hillside, a word was spoken to someone unseen and they squeezed through. "Follow," said the guide.

The way was cramped. A low passage led gently downwards into a large circular chamber lit by candles. The place was warm and dry, built with hewn stones to a height of twelve feet and roofed with slabs of black slate on old timbers. The walls were pierced by oblong alcoves and in them men sat or lay. Somewhere a jew's harp strummed a quick hillman's dance, a gilliecallum. Alastair knew he was in a burial chamber, a large one fit for a prince or even a king.

"Sit ye doon friends. Welcome to the Hill of the Fairies." The words came from the darkest corner of the tomb. The speaker's tone was deep and resonant and as his eyes adjusted to the light and shadow Alastair saw a man sitting in a crypt, his feet dangling. He was dressed in homespun and festooned with weapons, dirks, sgian-dubhs, a wicked looking long-handled spiked mace and a broad-sword which lay across his knees, blue steel glinting in the candlelight. He was the smallest man that Alastair had ever seen.

"I am Angus Mor," the little man boomed. "I am called Mor, the Great, and what I lack in stature I achieve in reputation. I enjoy the respect of brave men and in return I esteem courage. That is why you are both here in the Hill of the Fairies." They felt his appraisal. "You say you are the enemies of James Stewart of Garth yet you have walked into the den of the Accursed Whelp and come out unscathed. That is remarkable is it not? You have asked my clan to help you and we have done what you required of us. Now I am going to hear your story." Hogeston knew the Celt well enough to recognise the threat which Angus Mor had hidden in this apparently friendly welcome. Since Jean and he had left Aberfeldy there had been surprises for which the McIver now required an explanation.

"Very well," replied Alastair, "You shall hear my tale." There was a contented sigh and a rustling as men settled themselves to listen. Except perhaps for a fight, nothing in the world pleases a Scot more than a good tale well told, sung or recited, and the longer the better.

When he had finished, his audience, pale faces framed in dark holes, was still. He had omitted nothing and occasionally Jean had enriched an episode by her lively humour.

"What was it Sir Philip Hogeston did at Lochindorb to arouse so much hate and to merit such a death?" The McIver posed the inescapable question and once again Alastair was faced with the enigma of the unexplained. To McIver and his men he said quietly, "Witchcraft." In the tomb, the silence was total as they waited for him to continue. "James Stewart's father, the Wolf of Badenoch, believed that Philip Hogeston, the priest of Lochindorb, had practised the black art and bewitched his woman Mariota the mother of James now called the Accursed Whelp." A chorus of "Ah" filled the room. No other explanation was required. If they had to choose between the Christ teachings and the ancient superstitions they might accept the miracles but would fear the wrath of older Gods and all around the tomb there was a movement as men crossed themselves to ward off the Evil One.

Jean and Alastair slept fitfully, disturbed by the snores of the clansmen and the ghosts of the ancients. When they awoke they were alone with the man who had met them on the moor. The air stank of human fetor and the smoke of guttered candles. Outside their eyes hurt in the brilliance of an August morning. They mounted and rode for Perth.

"I am glad you used the story of witchcraft to satisfy Angus Mor," Jean said. "When did you hear of that? I didn't think you knew so much."

"I have remembered a lot since Garth," Alastair replied. "I heard the warlock story at Plewlands but I canna mind who told me." He looked puzzled. "Unless it was Catherine. Her head is full of kelpies and bogles."

"Mercy man," said Jean, "Did you not ken of the row between mother and Peter Grant's wife? I got it out of sister Catherine only by swearing on the Rood I would tell no one, but father's death releases me from that bond. Catherine asked mother one day what had happened at Lochindorb before father's escape and told her that Annie Grant had said father had practised witchcraft with Mariota Athyn the Wolf's mistress. Mother got very agitated, said it was a wicked lie and sent for Annie. Catherine told me she marvelled that Annie Grant was still at Plewlands. She was fleyed alive by mother's tongue."

Brother and sister rode silently, their horses picking their way by a burn which chuckled under ripening rowans to the water meadows of Strath Bran.

"And the other explanations Jean?" Alastair gave her a sideways glance. "Do you think there is a grain of truth in what James Stewart believes?" Jean ducked under a branch, pulled her horse up sharply and spoke as if to herself. "Poison, Stewart said and adultery. No matter what the temptation I cannot see father ever becoming a poisoner. Mariota maybe, but to what end? If she killed the Wolf, she would become a nobody, unmarried and unmarriable with five sons and a daughter to wreck her hopes. She would have to be mad to do such a thing."

"Could love not make her mad?" asked Alastair. "Mariota Athyn by all accounts was an unusually beautiful woman. What we have been told of her husband The Wolf does not flatter him – ugly, wilful, selfish, brutal, a man who took his pleasures where he found them with little respect for the feelings of his lawful wife and probably less for those of his mistress. Father on the other hand, a handsome young fellow of twenty, might present just the sort of challenge and infatuation to a woman in her late thirties, beautiful and deprived."

Jean looked at him in astonishment. "Depraved, you mean, if by your way of reasoning she poisoned one lover to make room for another. By the Grail Alastair, you have an imagination."

"Surely, Jean you must believe it possible for father to have fallen in love with Mariota? Remember how James described her."

"Indeed I do," said his sister. "Fallen in love, as you romantically call it, bedded with her, but mark you, only possible with the conniving help of Mariota herself. And that, my brother, is the vision which has festered in James' soul for forty-seven years!"

Alastair thought carefully about what Jean had said. The picture in his mind's eye of his father, the conventional one, was blurred and beside it another image had become more distinct, the shameful erotic boy-dream image of Mariota Athyn. He could understand James Stewart's murderous obsession and a small shudder of foreboding reminded him that his hate was now directed at him.

By the time they arrived in Perth he had selected the course he knew he must hold. In the monastery of the Black Friars he knelt before the altar where the Wolf had made his peace with God and swore he would slaughter James Stewart of Garth or die pursuing his revenge. But first he owed it to Bridget his mother to tell her how Sir Philip had died.

Nineteen

The Bluebell put to sea on the midnight ebb from Broughty Ferry and scampered north. By noon the breeze freshened and the dunes of Rattray Head flung their sand clouds like a scarf over St. Coombs. Jock Lorimer, her skipper, had intended to run her before the wind ten leagues north before heading south-west into the Moray Firth. But his only paying passenger was in a hurry and talked him into taking the shorter reach close to the shore.

"The man's daft," thought Lorimer. But he was being well paid so he set the Bluebell's head west when they passed the Broch and brought her into the Firth. It was a difficult course to hold. The little vessel lifted and plunged with the wind on her beam. The tide was flowing and her drift north was checked but she wallowed badly in the troughs. The helmsman, a big Hollander, swore continuously in Scots and Dutch, leaned his bulk on the long tiller and strained to hold the ship on course.

Hogeston, balancing himself on the poop, hung on with feet and hands and wished he had let the captain have his own way. After their argument Jock Lorimer had roared directions to the helmsman and stumped forward to his quarters in the fo'cs'l. That was the last they saw of him. The huge cliff of Troup Head passed slowly astern followed by the black teeth of Portsoy and later the white breakers on the Covesea Skerry. Long rollers, torn open by the reef, flung spray high in the wind. Hogeston recalled a story told him as a boy about another ship and another captain who had strained to clear those rocks and failed, a treasure ship which had broken her back and was rolled by the storm on to the yellow sands in the Bay of the Primroses. Gripping the rail, his hair matted with spume, Alastair Hogeston thought of the warm snugness of their room at Plewlands where, curled on the hearthrug with the dogs, Jean and he had listened in delicious horror to the story of that shipwreck. Their mother made a good tale of it. There was the finding of the Bishop's gold in the cave below the sea, a fight at the Bay of the Primroses, and the ambush of the raiders by young Philip Hogeston, at the Long Steps. That had been his father's first violent encounter with the Wolf of Badenoch. Now as he clung to the rigging with the wind tearing at his clothes and the green sea thudding and rushing on the deck at his feet, he thought again of his dead father and wondered as so often he had, about the strange position Philip Hogeston had occupied in the wild Stewart family of Lochindorb.

When the Bluebell cleared the sharp rise of the Broch of Burghead and tacked steadily towards the mouth of the Findhorn river he was joined on deck by Kenneth Fraser.

"Thon was the nearest thing to death I'll ever know," said Fraser. His face had the greenish tinge of the sea-sick landlubber. "I've spewed like a gull since this bloody ship butted into the Firth and all I want now is to feel good earth under my feet. Nothing will persuade me to leave land again."

Her sail reefed, the ship slid into the estuary on the tide and found slack water by the jetty. The sea journey had been fast, three days quicker than on horseback, but tiring. They hired garrons and made for the Crook of Alves then north to the loch of Spynie. The tide was in and from the slopes of the hill of Ardgye the two horse-men looked over a pale plate of water to the wood of the Keam glowing in the setting sun. The marsh sedge was heather purple and the home of noisy flocks of starlings. They met the bridlepath near the island of Starmoss and rode through flickering gold of birch trees to the Long Steps. The tide was on the flood and the brackish waters of the loch sucked quietly at the pillars of the old stone causeway. A cloud of starlings racketed upwards from the reeds, faded, formed and faded, performed their complicated precise manoeuvres then poured like black sand into the bulrushes.

"It's grand to be home," laughed Alastair. "The loch never changes yet it is never the same. I see that the Earl is in residence." A flag fluttered from the battlements of Duffus Castle. "He will have a hunting party from Stirling or Edinburgh and what sport they will have with their falcons." Swans, mallard, goldeneye, teal and pintail cruised in flocks on the broad waters and near the causeway cormorants dived at the sound of horses.

They rode to the castle and identified themselves to the garrison commander, then Fraser went north through the oaks to his sister's house in the village and Hogeston turned his horse towards Plewlands. The comfortable feel of home was all about him. Here was the gnarled tree as old as the Long Steps in whose heart Jean and he had built a tree-house. There was the glade where he had shot his first deer. He stopped his horse and stared into the forest as he had stared on that May dawn and felt again the jolt in his breast when the buck had walked from cover to the huntsman's call. Seventy paces from him it had stood motionless, ears pricked, sharp six-point antlers threatening its unseen rival. Alastair felt again the slow strain on his arm when he pulled the big bow and the faint tremor in his left wrist which he fought to control. The buck had seen him, but too late heard the zip of the arrow as it flew to its heart.

The oaks and the tall yews stopped suddenly as if afraid to go on. Hawthorn, heavy with claret berries crowded forward towards a walled fruit garden and rich green pastures wrested from marshland. Beyond, yellow in the slanting September sun, stood Plewlands with its turrets and blue-grey roof of Caithness slate. He rode slowly across the open field savouring the warmth of homecoming and dreading the chill of the tale he had to tell. Someone had seen him for as he approached a figure stood at the top of the flight of steps which climbed to the main door of the house. He knew it was his mother. He dismounted, straightened his clothes as he always did self-consciously in her presence and leaped up the stair. With a hug and a whirl he had her off her feet and was murmuring phrases he had used as a boy.

"Mamman, ma jolie mamman. Comme je t'aime."

He released her and looked at her, holding her by the shoulders at his arm's length. She was clothed in brocade the colour of Tokay which flowed from her pale shoulders to slim waist and over rounded hips to her tiny feet. Auburn hair with just the faintest suggestion of silver framed her face but the rich glory of it was half concealed by a head-dress of magnolia silk. Her calm warm eyes smiled up at him.

"Alastair, my little boy." She studied his face carefully, looking for the well remembered features, the high cheekbones and tiny laughter lines. The chin dimple was hidden by a brown beard that had been pale down when she had seen him last.

Then she stiffened and all happiness left her face.

"He is dead. I see it in your eyes." The soft French vowels tore at Alastair's heart. O why, why, had it taken this tragedy to bring him home?

"Oui, mamman, papa est mort," he said simply.

She gave a long sigh then stepped forward and took him by the arm. "You will tell me all, mon fils," she murmured. "I have known in my heart that I would not see him again in this life. But come, you are hungry and oh how dirty. The years do not change you, Nicky." Alastair looked at her and smiled. "I have been called that only once since I left home," he said, "by Jean and not so long ago."

"Well you are back again," she replied. "How is Jean?" She stopped. "No, you can tell me all I want to know later – Jacques!" An elderly, fresh faced man appeared from the house.

"Take this grimy fellow and scrub him clean." She hugged Alastair's arm, "Come to my room and tell me the tale while you are eating."

Later, as Alastair Hogeston walked down the corridor, music rippled from the half-open door of the room known in the house as mother's room. He stopped and listened. The cadences of a bitter-sweet Celtic air sang their way into his heart. It was a song they had learned as children, a lilting melody of long sea lochs, the croon of seals, the tinkle of mountain streams and the searching sough of wind on heathery hills. Lady Bridget had mastered the Gaelic harp very early in her Scottish life and as the children came she learned or composed a new tune to play to each of them. When they squabbled or fought or sulked, she would pick up the little harp and draw out their discord as she plucked harmony from its strings. As in the old days, the sound of the clarsach pulled Alastair into the room. The instrument rested between the long smooth curves of her legs. Her hair glowed like polished copper and long white fingers plucked and flowed over the strings. Softly she crooned an ancient love-song.

He sat in his father's curved beechwood chair and watched her. In all his life he had not seen her so beautiful. The slim woman who drew these breathless notes from the harp looked deceptively fragile and vulnerable. Yet she had cared for her five children alone when her husband was away at war in France or in Ireland or on the Scottish border. When Death's axe fell on her two eldest sons at the Battle of Harlaw she had nursed her grieving Philip through the terror of a hundred Hells. Now, she was facing the cruellest test to her strong spirit, her husband's murder far from his home and from her, in glaur and rain at the Bridge of Awe. Alastair knew with a shock that this soft sad melody was being played to soothe no quarrelsome child but that with every note she reminded herself of Philip her husband and rekindled her memories of him to red-heat. The music rose to a crescendo then ceased abruptly, as if unfinished, on the clash and question of a minor chord.

She raised her face and in the yellow lamp-glow Alastair saw the glisten of tears. "I must know everything," she said. Her voice was urgent. "Leave out no detail, spare me no anguish. Peter Grant when he dragged himself home on his wounded legs, told me of the conference in Stirling Castle with Livingston the governor and about his suspicions that some plot was hatching. He told me of the ambush by a black knight at the Bridge of Awe, and that Sir Philip had recognised his old adversary, James Stewart of Lochindorb. Peter was certain that his master had been slain. Then your message arrived. How was it that he survived?

Who cared for him and how did he die? Finally I want to know all that you can tell me of James Stewart of Garth."

Alastair Hogeston described the crowded events of the past weeks just as he had described them to Jean but with even greater emphasis on small detail and on timing. He knew in advance the things his mother would demand to know. So important to her was this final chapter in the life of her beloved Philip that every word spoken, every nuance of expression, every splash of boot or hoof in muddied waters, had to be described and explained. He suggested the plot he believed Livingston to have conceived, of using the ambush at the river Awe as his excuse for seizing James of Lorn, the Queen and the young King. He described the rough delivery of his wounded father to Dunstaffnage and how Queen Joan had nursed him back to the brink of recovery. He told his mother how he had tracked the Stewart force to their lair in Ben Alder, of his alliance with MacDonald of Glencoe and of his return to Lorn where he found the Royal family kidnapped by Livingston and his father murdered. Finally he described his meeting with James Stewart the Accursed Whelp in his castle at Garth. Through all, his mother sat still and quiet, her eyes on his face. At last she spoke and her words splashed into the silence that hung between them like trout rising in a moorland loch in the silver hush of dusk.

"Peter Grant has selected and trained ten of my best horsemen. He has, on my command, sworn each to secrecy as it is imperative that no whisper of our intention should go ahead of us to warn the enemy. The castle people here are my friends but they are also distant blood relations of the Stewarts of Garth and are not to be trusted with our purpose. Surprise must remain an ally. If you have no plan, prepare one now. My husband's murder must be avenged and swiftly. You must have no doubts as to what you must do mon fils." Alastair Hogeston looked at his mother, the gay compassionate Bridget who used to tease laughter from her solemn son and set his small world dancing. Her face now was beaten bare by grief as a blacksmith's hammer flattens the glowing iron. A stranger sat before him and in her eyes he saw the savage will that sustained her ancestors through a hundred years of war. Telling the tale of his father's murder he had heard his sister urge him to spare his mother nothing. "She will demand to know even the colour of the last stone you dropped on his grave," she had said. Now like Jean, Bridget was the implacable enemy of James son of the Wolf and searched the future only for her revenge.

Twenty

As the emerging may-fly dimples the surface of a small pool so the news of Alastair Hogeston's return to Plewlands occasioned a ripple of interest. Bishop Winchester sent his personal boat to ferry him across the loch to Spynie Palace. A friend of Philip Hogeston, he had done his best to comfort Lady Bridget when Peter Grant had brought her the news of the battle at the Bridge of Awe, and he guessed the reason for Alastair's homecoming.

The castle folk too, when they had expressed their sympathy, picked his brains on the complexity of Scottish politics. Everywhere folk were willing the blood-stained years of the King's minority to pass quickly but those closest to intrigue in the capital had to see to it, as they valued their lives, that their connections with the powerful were not compromised by events. The Earl's hunting party was from Edinburgh. They brought with them tales and scandals of the court and the latest information about the fate of Queen Joan, the Black Knight of Lorn and the young King James II. After the Royals were kidnapped by Livingston at Dunstaffnage, or 'rescued' as the Regent would prefer it, they were taken to Stirling Castle. There on August 3rd Joan saw her husband James Stewart of Lorn, together with his brother, led in chains to the dungeons. The young King was taken from her and Queen Joan, tearing at her captors with her nails and her teeth, was forcibly isolated in her rooms.

A month later Bishop Winchester had fresh news of the Queen. On August 31st the Regent had brazenly produced her before an assembly of the Estates where she was reported to have 'excused' Livingston's 'mistake' and graciously praised him for 'loyal' efforts on her behalf and of her son King James. She was thereafter united with her husband but lost the custody of the boy King. Alastair was in the Bishop's company when he heard of this. John Winchester, a fiery little man who wore thick soles to increase his height, exploded with rage.

"The traitorous rogue," he shouted. "Have I not known Queen Joan as long as any man in Scotland? Did I not escort her with her husband the King from his captivity in England?" He turned to Hogeston. "Your father and Lady Bridget were with us then. Does not Lady Joan Beaufort, the Queen, possess, as well as beauty, the rage of a panther? Did she not use tortures unheard of in this Kingdom, to wreak her revenge on her husband's murderers? Is it conceivable then that this noble tigress would suppress the truth about Livingston's treachery?" The little man stopped pacing around the room and turned to Alastair. "Bloody blackmail," he shouted. "For the price of the life of James Stewart of Lorn that worm Livingston had humiliated the proudest woman in Europe and forced her to lie!"

Later, when Alastair thought he knew Winchester well enough he told him, "I have become involved in a duel to the death with James Stewart of Garth. There is no doubt he means to kill me and I have done as much as I can think of doing to assess his competence in that matter and his determination. Both are unquestionable. His feelings toward my family are those of a man with insatiable hatred. He has a lunatic intoxication with murder. Explain to me Bishop if you can, the source of that man's malice, why Stewart of Garth third son of the Wolf of Badenoch and the beautiful Mariota Athyn, should believe my father to have been a poisoner, and adulterer, a warlock?"

The Bishop looked at him, astonished. A slow flush coloured his face and he turned away. He walked to the west window in the room and looked out over the fields and woods to the cloud-shadowed uplands and the faraway hills of Badenoch. Without turning he said, "All men have their secrets, come dark, most grey. They are secrets because they would bring distress to someone if they were revealed, or discredit to him who harbours them. Strangely, most secrets – and I have been burdened with many in my career as confessor – most secrets can be told openly and without dishonour after, for we are all the prisoners of our secrets, after their prisoner has died. There are things that you do not know concerning your father, things you would not understand, and you have shown to me that there are things which you suspect about him and are even prepared to believe. There are also things which I know and cannot divulge, on my professional honour as a priest, for the friendship I bore to your father and the respect I have for your mother, until my generation has filled its graves." He turned then and faced the only surviving son of his dead friend Philip Hogeston.

"Alastair," he said, "In your quarrel with Stewart of Garth there is nothing more you need to know about your father. James Stewart, the Accursed Whelp, is not so named without good reason. He will die unmourned. What he believes about your father is what he has believed since he was a child and a child, especially a boy child, plucks hatreds as he plucks apples and feeds on them greedily. James knows, for he was there with him when he died, that his father, Alexander Stewart, Wolf of Badenoch was a broken man, broken I would like to believe, by the fear of God. Timor Domini initium sapientiae. But I admit that I suspect other forces to have played their part in his capitulation, aye and in the bitterness of his death. I would confirm two of your suspicions if I denied only one of them. Poisoner? Adulterer? Warlock? One of these your father may have been. The other two, never. I know only what he chose to reveal to me. Of the total truth I may live and die in doubt!"

Ripples spread themselves in all directions and Alastair waited full of hope for stirrings from another quarter. Beatrix Sinclair lived in Duffus. She was rich, beautiful in a Roman way and Alastair had courted her before he left for Edinburgh. Their love affair had been ardent and only Sir Philip's insistence that his son, "must make something out of his lazy life", had pulled them apart. Beatrix fretted at home for a time then packed her bags and boarded ship at Findhorn for the capital and her Alastair. The sea-trip to her was a romantic gesture until gales five miles east of Girdleness ruined her complexion and cooled her passion so much that she begged to be put ashore. As she paid well the captain laid his ship alongside the wharf at Aberdeen and Beatrix's elopement was ended. That was months ago and since then Ola's sparkling eyes and ready charms had largely healed Alastair's heart. He remembered the letter Beatrix had sent to him on her arrival home from her aborted sea voyage. "If you want me you must come and woo me. Never again shall I set foot beyond a harbour wall, for you or anyone." She was still unmarried and fancy free and Alastair, after two months of abstinence, ached for her. In a very direct way Lady Bridget warned him to beware of entangling himself again with Beatrix Sinclair. "She" – Bridget never referred to her by her name – "She goes on heat like a bitch. It is a pity she has not what she deserves. Brats around her feet would take some of her thoughts from l'amour et les hommes." So Alastair waited impatiently for her next oestrus.

Beatrix heard of Alastair's arrival home almost as soon as his mother. Her sister Helen was linen-mistress at the castle, a strategic position for one whose family fortune was founded on a cloth-weaving business in Elgin. As soon as he arrived, Alastair sent a letter telling her that he had missed her sorely and was longing to be with her again. To this she replied, "It is now nearly five months since I saw you and my figure is as neat as ever. Your virility is therefore in doubt although your vigour was never in question. Perhaps you will be given another chance to prove your manhood. I will think on it. Beatrix."

A week passed while Alastair chafed and hoped. Then came another letter.

"I know your mother does not trust me – and why should I blame her. I shall follow my father's cattle to Starmoss tomorrow early." On the shores of the loch of Spynie are some choice pastures where the starmoss grows. These are on holms or islands and after the passage of the spring tides, cattle, weak from poor winter feeding, are driven across the shallows to gorge themselves on the new growth.

Alastair remembered Starmoss well. It was one of the larger islands in the western shallows of the loch and was surrounded by shingle. Two or three fir trees grew on it, broom bushes, hazels and in September a mass of purple willowherb floated twisted gossamer into the autumn breeze.

A sea fog lay cold on Plewlands. It moved like smoke through the tops of the oaks and laid a heavy dew on the pastures. Alastair rode between the village and the castle and took the right fork at the Long Steps. The track meandered through pines towards Spindlemuir and water gleamed between the trees. A cattle trail on the dewy grass stopped at the loch's side and he drove his mount towards the island. His mare was nervous at first as she sank knee-deep in mud but became bolder when she felt the firm crunch of pebbles beneath her hooves. On Starmoss island, he dropped to the ground and sent her off to seek the sweet green herb as her reward.

The heat of the sun lifted the haar from the willows, like steam. Beatrix was seated on the dead stump of an ancient oak in a bower of hazel trees.

"Aye," she greeted him, "Ye are the same handsome brute I remember." Alastair looked at her and she smiled back with her eyes. "Come and kiss me then or have ye forgotten what it's like to hold a lass to your heart!"

"I've been no priest since I saw you last Beatrix, but you are still the finest looking quine I've met in the last five months."

"Five months it is, but you'll have forgotten last Christmas in the gay life you live in Edinburgh."

"Lassie how could I ever forget thon Christmas when your face was coloured by rosy lust like an August sunset. I remember the taste of your breasts, the pale softness of your thighs, your greedy kisses and it's pleased I am to find you as bonnie as ever."

Beatrix laughed. "That's my man. I never lay with a lad who can talk like you. Kiss me, and syne we'll light a fire and heat some broth. Losh it was cauld this morning but I had to wade the cattle over early before someone else had the same idea. Not since I was a quine wi bare feet have I followed the kine and the devil of a row there will be if my father hears that his daughter was driving beasts like a common serf. Starmoss is well kenned by both beasts and lovers, but now the herd is on the island there is nane will disturb us."

They gathered driftwood, piled it in the hot sun to dry and lit a fire with dead leaves. They found a soft mossy hollow under the willows with a glimpse toward the pebbly shore and the burnished silver of the loch beyond. Beatrix was in no hurry. "It's all very well for you but I'm not for a wet bum so we'll wait a while till the grass dries."

They wandered, arms entwined, over the little island and fed each other with brambles that grew like purple grapes in thickets. Then, wrapped in plaid, they lay together. "Listen to him," said Alastair lifting himself gently on to her. Down on the shingle shore a herring gull, still resplendent in his courting colours, moved on top of his mate and the silence was filled with her encouragement and his raucous laughter as he flapped himself into ecstasy.

"I can do better than that mewling hen," said Beatrix, "But laugh like yon, my loon, and you'll get neither front or back of me again!"

Twenty-One

Alastair crossed the loch of Spynie not only to visit Bishop John Winchester but to see his sister and her family. Catherine was born three years before her brothers John and David were slaughtered on the Field of Harlaw and she was four years older then Alastair.

In his youth there was not much he could happily remember about his big sister and many things he preferred to forget. Jean, his junior by two years, had been his favourite, his chief companion and conspirator. Catherine encouraged the gap in their ages and preferred to act more like an aunty than a sister. When Alastair reached an age to judge these things, it seemed that she was determined to become a nun. She was, or appeared to be, a straightforward young woman, a prude and devoted to good works. She helped to look after her brother and sister, tidied their rooms, wiped their noses, and regarded her father in the rainbow light in which daughters not uncommonly place their male parent. In his role as a soldier of Christ he appeared to her in glowing colours. He had fought for the Faith at the sack of Elgin Cathedral and in the Crusade against the infidel Turk. But he slid into the purple and the blue when she tried to imagine her Sir Galahad at Lochindorb. The stories she had heard were so conflicting and even when she pressed her mother for the truth she had been palmed off with evasions. She could not understand why he had spent two years in the Wolf's fortress without trying to escape and his deliverance when it came at last was marred by his disappearance very soon after. She suspected that some heavy cloud hung over his departure to Rhodes with the Knights of St. John and she could not discover why. Catherine would have wished his homecoming to have been acclaimed by all, including the Church, as a victory of Good over Evil.

Being Catherine, she probed and puzzled and questioned. From Peter Grant's wife Annie, a big broody woman with ten bairns of her own and three more adopted, she had heard the whisper of witchcraft associated with the name of Mariota Athyn and the sulphurous stink of Hell exuded from that woman who Catherine believed, had encouraged the young priest of Lochindorb to indulge in nameless things. These pieces of 'information,' given to her in the spooky light of a flickering peat fire in Annie's kitchen, deeply influenced Catherine and were confirmed by an angry row between Annie and her mother. When, however, she told the Bishop at confessional what she had heard and what she thought, he had given her a penance for "impudent questioning about her devoted parents."

She loved her French mother dearly but was unable to love her father in the same way. She could not reconcile the image of a Knight of the Holy Grail, perhaps her father, with a copulating parent, certainly her father.

Fortunately for Catherine, John Stewart appeared in her firmament. He was a nephew of the Earl of Moray and godson of Bishop Harry Leighton and his uncomplicated zest for singing in the choir and fornicating in the straw of the castle stables finally convinced Catherine that the eternal and the earthly were not incompatible. They were married in the Cathedral and lived in a wing of the Earl's town house at Thunderton.

Alastair's first visit to them was to break the news to Catherine of their father's murder. In comparison to the trauma he knew he had inflicted on his mother, his interview with his sister was easy. She had been as prepared as Bridget had been for Philip Hogeston's death but either she lacked the imagination to comprehend the cruelty of his murderer or the compassion to weep for her father. Alastair was not too surprised by her lack of response. He had always thought Catherine as cold fish. But he did not forsee the attack she was to make on him, although he might have done had he remembered her contempt on another occasion many years before. Like most boys who see their pubic hair begin to sprout he had a special relationship at the age of twelve with two other lads. One was a cooper's son whose father's yard was a place of magic and adventure. Piles of unfinished, bottomless casks littered the back of the house and the boys built these into wells, dungeons, tunnels and castles. In the depths of this labyrinth of barrels and butts they had their den and it was there, with their breeks down and their hands working fast on their new spears that Catherine descended on them. Why a 'woman' of sixteen should have invaded this boy's world she never explained but she established a hold over her younger brother at that moment which she never relaxed.

When he was three years older he was caught by his sister Jean taking an educational interest in the private parts of one of the kitchen maids. Jean came on them in the pantry one afternoon when she was searching for something to eat. Dolina Maguire was lying on her back among the cheeses and the eggs with her knees up and her legs wide apart while Alastair, sitting between them, peered into her dark mysterious depths, encouraged by Dolina to "touch it there Ali, slow-like and gentle."

Jean giggled when she found them and said "Put your whole hand inside, Nicky. Dolly's parts are well used and big enough!" But that had been Jean.

Now, facing his older sister he felt the slow flush of ancient shame creep into his cheeks. She watched him keenly, then in words as light as cobweb and as hot as cinders, "surely you could have made better time from Stirling to the Bridge of Awe," she said, and, "What on earth were you thinking about to indulge in foolish heroics with good for nothing tribesmen in Glencoe when our father was in danger of his life at Dunstaffnage Castle?"

It was nothing new in the family to knock Nicky for his laziness but only Catherine could sprinkle poison on two such innocent questions. The cruel insinuation that by sloth he was responsible for his father's death took the wind and the bounce clean out of him. He left Thunderton House in low spirits and made straight for Duffus and Kenneth Fraser.

"I need to talk with you," he said as they rode up the high cliff-land behind the village and down to the green machair of Covesea. They left the horses to graze and climbed through the hills of sand to the miles of yellow beach between the dunes and the thundering surf.

"I have just been kicked in the balls by a woman – by my sister Catherine," Alastair began. "I want you to explain to me why I could not have reached the Pass of Brander and the Bridge of Awe before my father did and why our decision," he emphasised the pronoun "our" "to join MacDonald in the affair at Ben Alder should have taken precedence over my return to Dunstaffnage."

A cold northeaster whipped spray from the roaring sea and sand from the crouching dunes. The two men retraced every mile of their journey from Edinburgh to Ben Alder and back to Lorn. An hour later they stood together with their horses and Alastair turned to his companion. "What you have not done, Fraser, is to convince me I made the correct decision when I accompanied MacDonald to the Rannoch Moor. What you have done is to make me think that Catherine was right about me and that as usual I wasted time that my father sorely needed."

"Michty me," said Fraser. "You are ower hard on yersel maister. It was on my advising we accompanied the Badger to Ben Alder. Ye are welcome to mak me your whipping boy if it does you ony good, but mark my words, had we not helped these Westerners, we could expect nae favours from them ever again and on our own, what chance hae we against the Accursed Whelp?"

They mounted and rode side by side through the bare oaks towards Plewlands. "You told me you were weaned in Glen Truim", said Hogeston. "Would you still know your way about in those hills?" "I am sure I would," said Fraser. "I hunna been there for fifteen year but Glen Truim winna change much in centuries. Why do you speir?"

"I want you to go there and arrange a watch on Ben Alder. I have a strong feeling and so it seems have you, that James Stewart of Garth will raid the MacDonalds in Glencoe. He is not the man to overlook a defeat and will probably plan to settle that score before he turns his attention on me. You are right, we may need the help of the MacDonalds after all. Before I left Strath Tay I asked the McIver to get a message to Lady Jean at Megginch if Stewart moved west or north towards Glencoe. She will send word to me by boat but it could be many days before I know. There are two routes that Stewart may take. He could attack from the south through Glen Etive and will be sorely tempted to visit the meadow of Dierdre again. But to maintain secrecy and surprise surely his best route is by Tummel to Pitlochry and the Drumochter Pass to Ericht and Ben Alder. By now the bogs will have dried out and the going will be easy. When you have a definite sighting of the enemy make for Loch Ossian and warn Sam Cameron. He will put Glencoe on his guard. Keep well out of sight and let me know at once. Peter Grant has ten men chosen and ready to move fast. If nothing happens before the first snows then my guess has been wrong and you can return."

Fraser looked thoughtful. "Man," he said, "I only wish ye were as fast wi your sword as ye are wi your heid. Let me stay there a little longer. October in the high hills can be richt for horsemen when the ground is frozen. I can mind Glen Truim in late autumn. The rowans are red, a dust of snow flatters the tops, the lift is blue as a kingfisher's wing and the grun, iron hard wi' frost."

It was arranged. Kenneth Fraser went south into Badenoch that day with two young men of his own choosing and Alastair Hogeston prepared to wait. Some letters had arrived for him but none from Jean. Ola wrote him complaining that he had been away longer than "a few weeks" and how did he think she could live on what he had left for her. A very official document came from the Legal Department of the Realm relieving him of his commission – "Through prolonged absence from your place of duty and involvement with scurrilous banditry in the lands of Lorn." Alastair wondered how the commissioners had learned so much about him. He had more pleasant distractions. He went wild fowling in the early mornings, supervised the estate during the day, and saw more of Beatrix Sinclair than was good for either of them. Beatrix' oestrus was extended and passionate.

On the first day of October a message arrived from Kenneth Fraser. It was dated the 24th September. "Thirty horsemen from Garth arrived at Ben Alder today. They are equipped for a long stay and carry two heavy ordnances, probably Flemish cannon. I have not yet identified Stewart, but his son John Gorm is here." Alastair had only seen these infernal machines fired once when a battery of six was tested at Duddingston Loch near Edinburgh. Although one had blown up and killed its crew the fall of shot from the others had been very impressive and surprisingly accurate. He thought of the valley of Glencoe resting temptingly and in fair view of bombardiers on the slopes above and knew that The Fierce Wolf was baring his fangs.

Twenty-Two

B eatrix conceived on the afternoon of the first of October in the quarryman's hut at Greenbrae. Her matings with Alastair had been lusty and frequent but as she watched him ride up the path which curved from the beach to the quarry she knew with sudden certainty that this would be their last and that it would happen. She shivered. She loved this man and it was not only lust for him that made her heart pound. She walked down the slope, aware of the effect her slim young body would be having on him, aware also of the ache high up between her thighs. He dropped from the saddle and scooped her into his arms.

They clung together in the purple sunset of their love-making willing the pleasure to remain and their ebbing passion swelled briefly to the sharp tang of seaweed and the suck and kiss of waves on the shingle shore. Beatrix moved free and sat up. Through the door she saw white horses rear and drown on a sea as blue as the Caithness hills.

"You are going awa then," she said. Alastair lay on an elbow and watched her. He had said nothing about the message from Kenneth Fraser and her tone was a statement not a question. "So ye ken. Losh! There's little I think that ye canna jalouse." He kissed her arm. "When we part I ride for Badenoch and Ben Alder. I've said farewell to my mother and at this moment my men are slipping past the castle by the Long Steps. Fraser has sighted the Stewart."

"Ye leave me with child," she said.

His face became still. "When did it happen?"

"Now, ye muckle sumph!" She laughed at his surprise and sprang to her feet. "Ye've telt me o' the Wolf's bidey-in and her slinky dances. I've no chain o' gowd to woo my man's eyes to my belly but if that Mariota was swacker than me she maun be some woman!" She danced before him in the glim of the little hut, bare feet flashing on slender calves, her apple breasts bouncing in their frame of white arms and Alastair saw in this joyous urge her pride in her conception. He pulled her breathless to the floor.

"With all that loupin' about, if it hauds, the bairn winna ken its arse from its elbow! If I havna put a brat inside ye it will not be for want of trying. Lassie, gin I'm nae here when its born, ca' the laddie Philip and Lady Bridget's heart will melt to you."

"You'll tell her yoursel and dinna talk daft. God save me if I am left my lane but if you let me doon I'll mak thon high-born Frenchy mither o' yours ken she's a grannie and dang the scornlook frae her face!"

"S'truth!" Alastair exclaimed, "you would too for my bairn's sake."

"Your bairn! I'll never let him forget he's half Sinclair." She pushed her hand between his legs and giggled.

"The bigger half too by the feel o' this tired wee mousie!"

Hogeston left Plewlands that day. The Earl in Duffus Castle must not know that he was moving eleven well trained and armed men out of the district and to conceal their departure he sent each off separately with instructions to muster south of Forres and to stay clear of the castle at Darnaway. From there, they took the hill track by the Findhorn river and crossed the wide moors to Lochindorb where the castle, now a stronghold of the Black Douglas, floated on its loch, silent and grim. Alastair could picture his father, prisoner of the Wolf, being taken by the route he now followed, trussed up in a fowling net and slung on the back of a hill pony. Was it not prophetic, thought Alastair, that fifty years later he was in pursuit of his father's murderer James Stewart of Garth, the third son of Alexander Stewart of Lochindorb, Wolf of Badenoch?

When they rode higher into the hills fresh snow covered the

heather and big mountain hares, conspicuous still in their summer coats, jinked and danced on the powdery stuff.

"If these beasties are as plentiful and as easy to see on the Rannoch, we winna rin short of meat," remarked Peter Grant.

Ahead, the Cairngorm mountains thrust their white peaks into a sky of duck-egg blue. Alastair, plucking memories from his youth named them and the hill passes that split the range.

Old Peter was impressed. "Mercy master Alastair, I canna argue wi' ye but if ye're richt tell me how ye ken this wild land."

"I'm richt enough," laughed Alastair, "and there," he pointed left to a hollow in the hills, "there is Lochindorb, lair of the Wolf of Badenoch."

"Ye dinna say," said Peter in mock seriousness. "That wis my hame, man, for mony a year."

"Then you should know this country better than you seem to," retorted Alastair. "Your tales of raids on Forres and Elgin and your story of your escape with my father from yon place sent me riding up here, often alone, sometimes with Jean and Catherine and your own son Robbie. I got to know the old people who lived at the croft of Auchtertipper – look, there it is beside that patch of snow, deserted now unless the tinkers are using it."

"Less of the 'old', if you please," said Peter. "I kent them weel. Murdo McInnes and his wife Hilda are nae aulder than myself. Murdo was Alexander Stewart's right hand man, a cold calculating devil."

"Aye," said Alastair. "He was the Wolf's man and proud of it. He told me some strange things about my father, and he gave me the impression that the Priest and the Wolf were not unfriendly in a guarded sort of way."

"They were never cronies," laughed Peter. "I was in the kitchens except when on a raid, but Philip Hogeston was more often than not on good terms with the Stewarts – except for James. I mind how once he lost his temper with James and got spat on by that wild young tink! In the kitchens we thought your father saw ower much o' Lady Mariota, but no as much as he wanted to see o' Hilda. Hilda Macdonnell in those days was a peach of a lass and as Irish as they come. She had a twinkle in her eye that set the men puffing themselves up like blackcock in the spring. I mind on your father having it out wi' Murdo over the heads of Hilda. I didnae see the fight but it must have been a good one, because they baith limped aboot wi' faces like chopped meat for a month! By God she was a fierce kitten thon, and determined. I mind when Murdo met your father in the croft there at Auchtertipper. Sir Philip and I hadna long returned from the Crusade and he had been to Lochindorb to see the Wolf. I thought that was a wee bit strange, but he came back safe enough frae the castle and we went on to hae a word with Murdo and Hilda. There was something bothering your father and he trailed his coat before McInnes. He said something I canna mind on now, something insulting aboot the Wolf. Murdo went for him like a polecat and the twa wrestled on the kitchy fleer. Hilda stepped between then, as cauld as ice wi' a knife in her hand and threatened to kill the first who continued the brawl even if it was her ain husband. That sobered them up I can tell ye!"

They smelled the sharp tang of peat smoke from the hamlet of Kingussie at the same time as they saw Kenneth Fraser.

"Has Stewart made a move?" was Hogeston's first question.

"No," replied Kenneth. "The weather has changed. Heavy rain has softened the tracks and filled the bogs, and the Rannoch is a quagmire that will need a week tae dry oot."

"We are in time then," said Alastair. "These cannon are there to be used. Stewart will not advance on Glencoe without them and that must surely be impossible now?"

"True," said Fraser. "For the same reason I hiv nae been able to reach Loch Ossian to warn Sam Cameron that his enemies are near. And, by the bye, I've seen neithing of James of Garth."

They camped in a valley in the forest of Giack and set off for Loch Ericht early next day. With the fickleness of October weather in the high mountains the day dawned clear, the wind dropped and by late afternoon frost glazed the track with a quarter inch of hard ice. Thereafter the horses made good progress and they reached the cave on the south slope of Ben Alder by night fall.

"Kenneth," said Alastair, "Come with me to the corrie."

The two men climbed the crest of the steep bealach and searched the long valley. The moon in its first quarter shed a pale glim on the western wall and showed the loch lying like a black hole in the centre of the valley. There was no movement, no light, no sound. The two men crept down to the huts. No horse stamped a warning. No one was there.

"God, we must be a day late." Hogeston swore. "To be late has been the story of my life," he said. "We must get back and try to warn the MacDonalds before they are taken by surprise."

The moon hung low in the north-east and Hogeston knew that it was hopeless to follow that winding path through lightly frozen marsh in darkness. But they saddled up before dawn and were well into the moor when the rising sun pinked the snow-peaks of the Mamores. As the woods of Ossian came into sight they crossed the trail of the Stewarts. Grant studied the hoofmarks.

"James Stewart has spat in your eye again master Alastair. He has managed to drag the cannon with him." In confirmation they heard a sudden bang, weakened by distance but undeniably a cannon shot from the direction of Ossian. Then came a second and after a pause a third and a fourth. They heard men cheering.

"Stewart will be having target practice with Sam Cameron's house," Hogeston said grimly. His small troop rode up through the forest and on to the hill. Alastair and Peter Grant dismounted and looked down on the herdsman's home. It was in ruins, burning, and there was no sign of Sam and his family. They rode fast then for Glencoe and high on the Black Corrie they saw a horse. It was riderless and when they were nearly up with it Grant reined suddenly to a stop.

"Listen master," he commanded. They heard the thin wail of a baby and in an ice-filled peat hag they found it bound to the breast of Mary Cameron, who lay dead beside the body of her husband Sam.

Both had been shot in the back by a cross-bow. Fraser dropped from his horse and gently lifted the wee fellow from his mother's shawls. He was still warm and yelled in Kenneth's arms.

"Och ye puir wee man, your Mam and your Dad will never see you again but thank the Lord ye're alive and that we've found ye and not these bad devils." He looked down on Mary and Sam. "God rest their souls. I never would have believed sic a thing could happen to that muckle comic of a man and his douce wee wifie."

They marked the place of the dead with a cairn of turf so that MacDonald, later, might know where his daughter died. Then they tied the bodies on to the back of a horse and rode on to the mouth of Glen Etive.

"Ride to Glencoe, Peter. Alert the MacDonalds, and pray for rain to stop these war machines in their tracks. Fraser and I will take this wee cratur to the croft in the meadow of Dierdre. The women there will know better how to care for him."

"Nae need for me tae prod the MacDonald when he sees the face of his dead daughter," said Peter. "He will be on the road at the head of his clan before you are far doon Glen Etive. Can I expect you back to lead the attack or are you content to leave me in command of my own men?"

At the tone of his voice Alastair looked up sharply. He had sensed Peter's impatience since they rode from Duffus. The man was a veteran of war and resented his young master's assumption of command. He had sworn to Lady Bridget that he would seek out and destroy Sir Philip's murderer and return with her husband be he dead or alive. Sir Philip was now buried at Dunstaffnage and he had been made to feel his age by this youngster. Alastair flushed. Peter Grant was part of his life. He was his riding master and weapon instructor; always he had been his friend, faithful, dependable, much closer to him than his father. Suddenly he was embarrassed to be commanding this old crusader-warrior and for the first time in his life he felt awkward in Peter Grant's presence. He studied the wrinkled tense face, the grey beard, the sharp eyes with their white arches around the pupils and, with a shock, realised that Peter Grant had grown old.

"Peter," he said looking straight into his friend's face. "You are in charge now as you always have been. I know you believe you have the right to be my father's avenger and I am grateful to you for the love you have for him. Were he still alive I doubt if I could stop you. But he was my father and he is dead and I alone have to settle the score with James Stewart. Link up with MacDonald and I shall join you on my way back from Etive, and may God grant we meet up with the Accursed Whelp."

Peter Grant sat quite still on his horse for a few moments. "Very well master Alastair but no one will mak me leave your side when we face the enemy. The Stewart has me to settle with too." The Duffus troop trotted west along the hill track under Buchaille Etive Mor. Alastair and Kenneth cantered south down the Etive trail, Fraser with the small bundle in his arms that was the grandson of the Badger, chief of Glencoe, cousin to the Lord of the Isles.

Twenty-Three

Ian MacDonald turned his bearded face to the heavens when he saw his dead daughter and gave a great wailing cry that echoed to and fro among the mountains above the village. It was like the roar of a stag, a chilling sound that struck fear into all who heard it for it carried the tongue of grief and outrage. Every man who could bear a sword or pluck a bowstring rallied behind this giant of a man. Peter Grant found himself in the van of an army of seventy, mounted or on foot, booted or baretoed, who followed their chief with grim yet happy determination to slaughter the enemy. This motley force set out in the dark and when they reached the gorge of the river Coe the moon lit up the hillside to the north of the pass and the dense shadow of Stob Dearg hung like a curtain of concealment over horse and man. Once more the storm clouds had fled over the rim of the great wood and marsh of Rannoch and cold struck at the glen from the stars, ice sharp. Men could hear the crackle of frost as it came at them out of the black wastes of the sky and hastily wrapped strips of cloth round their feet and pulled their plaids over heads and ears.

"If they would come now we would have them," mused MacDonald. "But the beggar will not be so accommodating. Wheesht!"

The man stood stock still and listened. Hooves clattered over the stoney track ahead. Three riders came into sight and were in the midst of the waiting clansmen before they knew it. They were Aeneas MacDonald, Hogeston and Fraser.

"Ha Ha my bonnie lads you are not too careful. Have you seen aught of the foe?" The chief spoke in French in what he imagined to be a whisper.

"Indeed, do you think I would waste time when they are not two miles behind us," replied Alastair in the same tongue. "If you hold your breaths you may hear them, such a noise these infernal cannon are making on their carriages."

"Good," said the big man. "We shall sit here then and wait for them. They will be weary from the dragging and pushing and will never know how they came to be caught by the barefooted MacDonald. I would like to see the face of James Stewart when the first arrows fall on his men."

"John Gorm will be leading his father's force," said Hogeston. His voice was flat. "He may wonder why his father has not rejoined him but I do not doubt he will be glad to lead the expedition on his own."

"Why will his father not be here?" asked MacDonald, "And how are you so sure?"

Aeneas gave a single sob and fell at the feet of his chief. Men pressed close straining to hear.

"James Stewart, The Accursed Whelp will never join his son in battle again. He is destroyed."

Alastair looked the big man in the eyes. "It is so," he said. "He was mutilated this day at the croft of Aeneas in the meadow of Deirdre by Morag MacDonald."

An astonished "Oh" came from the shadowy listeners.

"He did not meet an honourable death but has been struck down in a manner which befitted him as a despoiler of women." Aeneas gave a cry. "God forgive my daughter."

"Your daughter needs no forgiveness from God or man," said Fraser. His voice was choked, his eyes wild in the reflection of the moon, "She has so marked the viper that he will never defile another woman. Morag MacDonald has given him his desserts." Then there was a pause. Spitting out his words the chief asked, "You speak in riddles, all of you. Out with it Hogeston. What is this thing that has happened at the croft of Dierdre?"

Seventy men huddled round the small knot of speakers as Alastair Hogeston faced their chief and began.

"Fraser and I rode down Glen Etive carrying your grandson. When we were below Stob na Broige I saw two people riding fast towards us and when they came nearer I recognised Aeneas here and my sister Lady Jean of Megginch. I had last seen her after our reconnaissance of Castle Garth.

" 'Alastair,' she cried to me. Her face was marked by some terrible grief or grievous sight and she wept when she saw me."

" 'What are you doing here?' I asked. I was bewildered." Alastair hesitated. "I shall tell you the tale MacDonald exactly as she told it to me," he said.

"Jean stopped weeping. 'I am glad to see you,' she said. 'I sent word to you when the McIver reported to me that James Stewart had left Garth with a war party and I followed them as soon as I could. The McIver helped me but I found myself on the trail of only one, the Fierce Wolf himself. He went by the Pass of Brander into Lorn and then to Glen Etive. I remembered your story,' she said, 'of the lust he had for Morag MacDonald and half expected to come upon him at the meadow of Dierdre'." Alastair cleared his throat. "Little did she know what she would find. When she turned the shoulder of the hill before the croft she heard a screaming and a shouting and saw Aeneas MacDonald leaping over the bog. Ahead of him a young woman, tearing off her clothes, ran like a doe towards the river's gorge. Aeneas was shouting 'Eilidh, Eilidh.' Then the child screamed and disappeared. She leapt into the cauldron pool."

Hogeston paused. "Well?" asked the Badger. Alastair sat down on a rock beside him.

"Jean rode hard for the croft and was met by Aeneas' wife shrieking, her eyes staring and near to madness. Inside the croft Jean found the place a mess of gore, on the walls, on the furnishings. In the middle of the floor sat Morag, stark naked, spattered with blood, rocking herself to and fro, laughing, laughing, mad laughter. Jean went into the other room, the sleeping chamber. James Stewart lay across the bed. He too was naked as God or the Devil made him and was staring at the roof, his face drained of all colour. His loins, his legs and his belly were royal purple, covered in the most gruesome paint of all. "Blood, blood, blood, nothing but blood." Alastair stopped speaking.

"So," said the Badger, rubbing his cheek, "The Fierce Wolf of Garth, The Accursed Whelp, is dead."

Aeneas turned and stared at his chief with shocked eyes.

"Dead! My God MacDonald. Lady Jean went to console my wife Agnes and to help her with Morag. When she steeled herself to go into that room again, it was empty. He was gone, dressed, mounted and away!"

Seventy men in the darkness growled their amazement and at that moment the enemy came into sight on the moonlit path below.

Twenty-Four

It is possible that the battle below Stob Dearg could have been fought that ice cold October moonlight night of 1440 and not one soul in the kingdom beyond Glencoe know aught of it. No whisper of disaster would ever come from Stewart lips, for only two were left alive to tell, John Gorm who was ransomed in secrecy and James Stewart of Garth who was never again seen outside his castle until he was carried forth to his grave. Or do I forget the bards of Clan Donald who, since the days of Ossian have set to stirring verse and song the deeds of their heroes? If so I, Jean Hay, do them less than honour. But in my soul I liken the saga of my Hogeston men to the ballad of King Arthur and his Knights. My fault, you see, is that I love my people. They have shortcomings but I love them the better for that. Their loyalty and their chivalry are without reproach.

The history of my brother's feud with James Stewart of Badenoch and Garth has been told to me by himself, by my mother, and by his companion and squire Kenneth Fraser. It was from Fraser at last that I learned how Alastair had died. Och, I had the bare bones of the matter out of him two days after the fight when he arrived at the MacDonald croft in Glen Etive but it took all my woman's wiles to goad him into talking freely about that swift midnight slaughter by the river Coe.

The stark tragedy that had fouled the meadows of Dierdre had loaded my thoughts with foreboding and I was at the door of that croft waiting with a heavy heart for news of the battle when two horsemen came over the hill. The posture of the leading rider, sitting high and firm in the saddle was in contrast to that of his companion who, slumped over his horse's neck, looked weary and woebegone. When hooves clattered over the bridge a bow's shot from where I stood I recognised Aeneas MacDonald and Kenneth Fraser. I was glad to see them alive.

"How is Morag, and the wean?" asked Kenneth.

"You will see for yourself," I said and knew then it was for Morag's sake he had ridden the long miles from Glencoe with his leg in bandages.

"Where is Alastair?" He slid from his saddle awkwardly, carefully turned his back on me and tethered his horse to the barn post.

"Lady Jean," he said, "Alastair was killed by John Gorm Stewart."

He must have been even more surprised than I was when I fell against his chest and blubbered my heart out, but he is a fine friendly fellow and women need such men to cry on. With Aeneas we went into the croft. Agnes MacDonald looked at us.

"So ye are baith alive." That was all she said, all the greeting she gave her man before she turned and threw some peats on the fire.

I felt sorry for Aeneas, the poor weak creature. He was brimful of pride and importance for the first time in his life, and aching to tell her that he had been at the slaughter of the Stewarts.

Kenneth strode over to Morag. She was sitting by the small window rocking in her arms the child of Sam and Mary Cameron. Ken squatted in front of her but Morag gave no sign that she had seen him.

"Let me have the bairn lass," he said. Morag handed him the baby and her huge brown eyes watched as he walked up and down in that small cottage with the Badger's grandson in the crook of his arm. He is a big man and with the tiny mite happy on his shoulder he filled the room. I knew then what was to be and sighed my relief that the wee orphan had found his foster-parents.

In spite of his wounded thigh Kenneth accompanied me the long miles to Strath Tay. He must have hated the journey. His leg began to swell the day we left Glen Etive and pained him for the rest of the way. And all the time he was thinking of Morag. I was poor company for him because my mind was numbed by Alastair's death.

"Alastair," my heart sobbed, "My pet, my only and dearest brother, I will never see you again and if the MacDonalds had not put you in the ground with their own dead the foxes and the hoodie crows will scatter your bones and the winter's snow will be your winding sheet." I grieved for my dead brother as I had never grieved for any one, not even my father. Kenneth was kinder to me than I deserved for during the five days it took us to reach Dunkeld my tongue was raw through biting on sorrow and I taunted him cruelly to break his silence. He had told me nothing of the battle in the moon's shadow of Stob Dearg. "Tell me about the fight in Glencoe." I said at last, "or is there something you prefer to forget, some disgraceful deed you dare not speak of, to me or even to yourself."

We were descending from Glen Ogle. In front of us, Ben Vorlich was painted on the smooth depths of Loch Earn. He reined his horse, looked at me steadily with his dog's eyes. "It is not possible for me to forget," he began. He had grown more like Alastair since the battle. He even sounded like Alastair except for the Scots burr that coloured his speech. "I was afraid and as in all moments when fear puts spur to the spirit I can remember clearly every shout as I stumbled down the heathery slope, every blow, every bestial face of foe and friend lit up by the moon as we stabbed and cut. The sounds and the sights of that night are stamped on the soil of my memory like the slash of a horse's hoof on ploughed earth." He was silent for some time before he spoke again. "The first that the Stewarts knew of the Badger's presence was when MacDonald's men zipped some arrows into the knot around the cannon. There was too little light for good shooting so we roared into the moonlight and on to our startled enemy. Malcolm was first to reach them, Malcolm who worshipped Morag and whose world, since Alastair had told his story in the dark hour before the battle, was foundering like a ship with its keel ripped off. Malcolm was the first to kill and the first of the MacDonalds to be killed. Alastair, close followed by Peter Grant, went straight for John Gorm. He fought him bravely but he was aye the better wi' words than wi' a blade. I saw him clash with the Stewart and saw the sword pierce him through. By God that man could fight. He leapt over your brother and ran straight at Grant and me, his sword whistling and he, yelling like a madman. We fell back, parrying his blows till MacDonald shouted 'Get that one alive,' and John Gorm was set upon by half the clan. He slew two men and maimed three including myself before he was taken." I saw Kenneth press his hand on his wounded thigh. "The rest of the Stewarts were slaughtered where they fought or where they lay. No quarter was asked, none given. The cannons were hauled off down the glen. They were their proudest prize. Even the capture of John Gorm took second place to these two long wicked iron devils. With twelve of the clan I had to be carted from the battle and I remember admiring that proud Stewart as he rode with MacDonald into captivity."

"What will the Badger, as you call him, do with John of the blue armour?" I asked.

"His father, Stewart of Garth, will ransom him," replied Kenneth. "And he will have to pay dearly. He can do no less, for if he lives, thanks to Morag he will sit like a eunuch in his lonely tower despised by men and shunned by women till the Devil drags him into Hell."

He spat out the words and I knew that he was thinking too of those other visits the Accursed Whelp had made to the croft in the meadows of Dierdre.

Twenty-Five

When Fraser and I reached Dunkeld, Graham met us with twelve armed men and when he saw me safe his handsome face was torn between anger that I had made him show anxiety and delight to find me unharmed. "Why for God's sake had ye to go visiting at Garth?" he exploded at me when he had first crushed me in his bear's hug. "When Maisie told me you were off on your own to stay with Janet Stewart I thought at first that it was a sly woman-device to cover up some peccadillo." He turned on Kenneth. "Who is this man?"

"This man," I said, "is Kenneth Fraser. He has had business with James Stewart and as he has been chivalrous enough to convey me here you can treat him with some courtesy."

On the way home I admitted that I had deceived him and told him the whole story of my adventures including the saga of Glen Etive. By the time we reached Megginch I had, I suppose wishfully, aroused his passion to boiling point. That night I fell with child. During my pregnancy I was permitted to do absolutely nothing and I wiled away the dull months by setting down on paper my memories and my thoughts about the murder of my father and the death of my brother. At first I jotted down only times and places and the names of people so that I should have these clear in my mind when I arrived at Plewlands. I had decided to make the long journey home to show off my new baby and I knew that my mother would ask the most searching questions and expect to be answered in the smallest detail. Only the bald news of Alastair's death in the fight at Stob Dearg would have reached her when Peter Grant returned.

When Yolette was nearly three months old and not yet weaned from her wet-nurse my family moved north. Graham came with us. He called me pigheaded and chickenbrained and railed at me for dragging him "into thon cauld wastes o' wind and weet at sic a season." It was late September, not, I knew, the best time to make the long journey round the mountains with my children and my baby but I was to spend Christmas with my mother at Plewlands. Bridget Hogeston has never asked me or anyone for help but she has her own way of getting what she wants. She sent me a letter just before Yolette was born, so full of stories about her grandson Philip and so empty of all I longed to hear of Beatrix Sinclair that not even Graham could have stopped me from going home. So despite the grumblings of their father the Hay family of Megginch trundled off to Moray. It was quite a cavalcade. Four children between the ages of seven and three months need an incredible number of things and my wet-nurse Maggie had her three bairns, which added to the fun. In all there were seven children and four servants. I would have taken five but Graham refused to include old Dooty. Dooty has been with us since we married and with me since I was born. During all that time she has used her loving but excoriating tongue to divert me from the marigold beds of self indulgence. I have never had much time for girls but I made time to be with the boys and I suppose Dooty thought the worst would happen. We had a fat bitch called Belle who was usually tied to the leg of the kitchen table during heat while all the stray dogs of the village fought and fouled outside. Mark the gardener drowned more puppies than we cared to remember. I was in the kitchen waiting for Dooty's hot pancakes to come off the girdle when I saw Belle the bitch lying on the floor fastened with the inevitable piece of tow to the table leg. "Och you puir cratur, what a shame to tie you up," I said. Dooty's back straightened a little and she thumped the dough hard with her rolling pin. She spoke to me over her shoulder, "Jean lass, ye wad be neen the waur o' being tied up yersel sometimes." She was now in her old age, a shauchly wee body with a humpty back and an acid tongue and I never really reckoned on persuading Graham to take her with us.

The weather was good and we arrived at Plewlands at last, our tempers frayed, but in safety. Graham stayed for five days, longer than he usually spent with his mother-in-law, before riding east to Aberdeen. He is fond of her but at Plewlands he finds himself on the defensive. He had, of course, slipped a bairn into me out of wedlock which did not endear him to Bridget daughter of the Compt de Dreux.

Graham had always enjoyed Alastair's company. They had the same smooth charm that won friends, especially women friends. He thought Alastair's skill at arms was laughable but he respected his ease of address and his quick repartee. I knew that he had often stayed with my brother in Edinburgh but I was careful not to enquire too persistently into the reason for these meetings although I had my suspicions. When I read to him Bridget's description of her first encounter with Alastair's love-wife he exploded in laughter and became more enthusiastic about our journey to Moray. And little wonder, for the drama, the impudence of the woman and her daring was astonishing.

"Elfin, je suis etonné par l'audace de cette coquette," Bridget wrote. "Sacre-Coeur! Elle a le toupet du diable!"

Beatrix had the wit or the cunning to name her baby Philip but in the six months which had passed since that extraordinary confrontation I wondered if Bridget Hogeston's heart had melted even a little to her impossible daughter-in-law.

After five days Graham packed his bags, made his excuses to Bridget, his peace with me and left.

"God," he exclaimed. "Plewlands is like a smith's forge. The sparks are flying and the heat is on. I'm awa tae see my faither. He's gey feel but no sae daft as thon twa."

To begin with there was no approaching Beatrix Sinclair. She clung to her baby and was quick to respond to the smallest slight. She is not only a pretty woman. She has that quality of character and bearing that men call beautiful and her sullen moods made her formidable. She is five foot nine inches tall, weighs ten stones and, as Graham impudently remarked, "Is all bum and bust." Her determination and her single handed battle with the powerful Hogeston-Hay faction caught my admiration. Graham annoyed me by laying a bet that she and I would be good friends within a month and of course he won, with a week to spare.

Twenty-Six

"There is a man and his wife with a child living in Duffus village whom you know," Lady Bridget told me one day. "I gave them a house when they came here in the spring time because the man had shown great loyalty to Alastair."

Thus it was that I discovered Kenneth and Morag and little John Cameron in a cot near the common ground which the villagers tilled behind the forest. I was surprised and pleased that they were so near to me and yet, as I rode through the woods, I knew that it was not only the desire to see them that made my heart race. What had happened at the croft of Dierdre was horrible indeed but in its telling it would be even more revealing. Some madness in me still slobbered wolf-like over the blood and nakedness of that awful scene.

It was the thirtieth day of September and the woods held their breath awaiting the gales of the equinox. Shafts of sunlight pierced their russet roof and drifts of crisp brown leaves softened the path. Two red squirrels raced across ground ivy and vanished behind an oak. The trees ended and I followed a straight path between the run-rigs and the village. Kenneth and wee John sat on a low dyke in front of a cottage sorting hazelnuts. In the sunlight Kenneth's fair hair outblazed the splash of scarlet berries on the rowan tree by his door. The wean was intent on picking ripe nuts from Kenneth's hand and dropping them into a vessel on the ground.

In time with the movement of his little fist Kenneth recited a fairies' song I remembered from my own childhood.

"Een, Twa, Three, Four
Leave a suppy by the door.
Five, Sax, Seeven, Eich,
For the fairies in the Laich."

My roan gelding blew gently through its nose and Kenneth looked up.
"Losh be here, it's Lady Jean," he said and picked the wee lad off
the wall to greet me.

I slipped from my horse and hugged the two of them.

"Where's Morag?"

"In the hoose making bramble tarts," he replied.

"Morag, come oot and see fa's here," and Morag appeared lissom
and bonnie as I remembered her, her black hair a-gleam in the
slanting sun.

It was wonderful to see them again and I returned often to their
little house. I sensed they were both pleased to see me and embarrassed
as well. Glen Etive was never mentioned but I was aware of a nervousness
in them every time I spoke. I could stand this barrier to our friendship
no longer and one morning I said, "Kenneth, di ye mind thon mad
October before ye got married when ye met me under Bauchaille
Etive Mor wi' this babe in your arms?"

An apple thumped on the grass and a robin piped his arrogant
little song. "Is it likely I shall ever forget?" he replied. He was ill at ease
but I plodded on. I recalled all that I knew of the death of my father
and of the events which followed. It must have dawned on him that I
had a good reason for talking thus but he made no response. Then
once or twice he corrected me, helped to fill in gaps in my knowledge
and, before he knew it, he was in full cry pouring out the story and
turning up memories as a ploughshare will turn up old bones long
buried. Morag joined us for a time before packing the youngster off
to bed. "There are things, wee John, ye are best not to ken," she said
and lifted him, protesting, from my knee.

When she had gone inside the house I said, "Has she ever talked of
the day she libbed the Stewart?"

"Not a word has she spoken of the croft in the meadows of Dierdre since I returned to Glencoe and made her my wife," he replied.

"Walk with me to Plewlands, Kenneth. It will be like old times." I smiled and put my hand on his arm. He called out, "I will see Lady Jean back to the Big Hoose, Morag."

We walked through the gnarled oak forest that has stood round Duffus since the days when the Viking settlers planted it to provide hulls for their long boats. The October sun slanted over the loch. The equinox had whipped most of the trees bare by now and crumpled leaves rustled under our feet. I spoke first. There was much I had to say to him.

"After I met you and Alastair that day on the Etive trail I returned as you know to the croft. My arrival with the child of Sam and Mary Cameron steadied the women. I gave him to Morag. She was still crying and laughing and rocking herself as she sat on the floor but she took the bairn and cradled him to her bare bosom. Then Agnes, without another word, fetched a bucket of water, cleaned the floor and the walls of the room where Morag and the Stewart had lain, remade the bed and with my help lifted the body of her poor drowned Eilidh on to clean linen. All the while she talked to the dead girl as if she were only sleeping. She prepared her, stopped her nose and mouth, combed out her tangled wet hair, and bound her stiffening limbs together. I remember every move she made; the quiet way she talked to the corpse of her child; how particular she was to have her looking pretty. Morag dressed herself while her mother and I worked on Eilidh and crooned a lullaby as she cradled the baby in her arms outside in the sun. Agnes remade the kitchen fire and when it was well lit she hung a pot on the chain and boiled some leeks – a dish I loathe but oh how welcome it was that night. No one slept. I was terrified by the thought of what could be happening in Glencoe. Remember, you were not far ahead of the Stewarts when you took the path down Glen Etive, and I had a premonition that death must spread his wings to Alastair and to yourself."

I gave his arm a gentle squeeze. "I am glad you were not killed, Kenneth. Thank you for returning so soon to the croft and for escorting me back to Strath Tay. You must have hated that journey what with your leg in bandages, me a blubbering wreck, and Morag farther from you with every long mile."

That was the first of many talks. I came one day with a box full of papers and spread them on Morag's kitchen table. "Kenneth," I said. "I have put down all we can recollect of the events of that year."

"Mercy, Lady," he retorted, "Why is it so important for you to write down these tales of lang syne?"

"Somewhere," I continued, "It must be here at Plewlands but I canna find it, somewhere there is a longer story than this written by my father and telling of the wild days he spent in Lochindorb Castle with the Wolf of Badenoch and his family. I believe that it contains the secret of Mariota Athyn's banishment and of the deeds that led to the curse screamed at Philip Hogeston by young James Stewart. That was the very beginning of the affair and I owe it to all who have died because of that curse to tell this story." I read him the account and when I had finished he sat silently watching me in his knowing quizzical way.

"Why look at me like that?" I said. "Have I not done it well? That is all there is to it. I can add no more."

"Yes you can Lady Jean." He spoke quietly. The moment had come. I stood up, looked round and saw Morag leaning against the kitchen dresser. Her hands were by her side and her knuckles showed white. "Yes you must Lady Jean," he said again with sudden determination, "For if you winna, someone else maun speak about it. Morag and I canna live any longer with this thing between us." He stopped. His glance was drawn to the object that hung at my waist, the thing that Morag could not take her eyes from. He said carefully, "Suppose you tell us where you got yon."

So they had both seen it, the gleaming snake of love-knots that hung around my hips and dipped to its wildcat clasp on the vee of my belly. I had no doubt that this fateful band of twisted gold had been part of the Bishop's treasure so long ago, the lure that had drawn Alexander Stewart the Wolf of Badenoch to face young Philip Hogeston's arrow at the Long Steps. It was the lodestone that pulled at the eyes of Mariota's lovers, and at my father's too, in Lochindorb. It had entwined Sir Philip's arm at the Bridge of Awe and for a time had stemmed his life's blood. And it had been worn by James Stewart the Accursed Whelp as he moved to possess Morag MacDonald at the croft of Dierdre. I had known when I fastened it to my waist that I was going to put the marriage of this man and this woman to a test that might destroy it and I had weighed that risk against the cancer of half-known things and of love made sour by silence. I had suspected, rightly it seemed by their reaction to the golden bauble, that between them stood an ogre who chilled their hearts and whose name was James Stewart of Garth. I countered his question. "Do you truly love your wife?" He tore his eyes from the wicked winking serpent and looked straight at Morag.

"I have loved her from the first time I saw her," he said, "when she walked beside her father at the croft of Dierdre with a bundle of driftwood on her back and a knife in her hand. . ." His voice tailed off. Morag stood as if turned to stone. Her gaze never left the cruel gems which were the eyes of the snake that entwined my stomach. When at last she spoke we had to strain to catch her words.

"I know where you got that. I saw it last where it had been dropped on the floor by the bed when I lay with Stewart." A sob racked her body. She said nothing for a time, then, "He undressed, wound that thing slowly from his arm, swung it from his finger and thumb, watching me closely; then he hung it between his legs and said, 'Take this off, Morag MacDonald, and you can wear it round your pretty neck'."

"I had known, when he entered my father's house, that I was going to murder him and I had made up my mind that I would kill myself whether I succeeded or not. I had a small sharp knife – a skiandubh – hidden in the bed where I could reach it when he lay with me, as I kenned he would. But when I saw that serpent dangling and heard it clink against his thighs I knew there was a better way to be revenged.

He watched me as I took off my clothes and lay on the bed. It had been hard and brutal rape before so when he saw me stretched there, ready for him, he gave a cry of triumph and fell on me like a frenzied bull. I let him start his plunging and then I pressed my hands hard against his chest. His bearded face grinned down at me as he shifted his weight, his breath rasping on my throat. I bided my time and at the moment when his eyes no longer saw, I brought the knife fast across his belly. He gave a shout, a scream of pain and I was out from under him, panting against a wall and watching the man writhing on the bed." Morag's eyes rolled upwards and she crumpled on to the floor. Kenneth leaped across the room, fell on his knees and lifted her against his chest.

"Morag, Morag, my own dear love," he cried, "It is fled, it is gone." He kissed the sweat from her ashen face. Her breath came back in slow sighs.

"She has never talked to you of this before?" I asked.

"Not once," he replied, his voice choked with emotion. "And I love her now as much for her courage as for her confession."

Morag stirred and opened her eyes.

"Aye, my bonnie man," she whispered. "And can ye love a woman like me as much as a man should love his wife or is the shadow of the Beast of Garth too big even for you?"

"Lassie, lassie, James Stewart is washed out of my heart and yours, by truth, exorcised and gone for ever." Tears ran down his big face as he cradled his wife.

I unclasped the golden band from my waist and dropped it into the pocket of my riding jacket. It had worked its cruel magic. I saw colour return to Morag's face as she slipped an arm round Kenneth's neck and wept her guilt away. I wondered what I should do, for the moment was precious to them. After a while I said, "Kenneth, you muckle stirk, you will fill her with your bairnies yet."

Morag looked up at me.

"I hope that will be so, and soon." She listened. A child's cry came from the other room.

"I could not have lived without my wee John Cameron," she said. "I love him as my ain, but I have longed to give this man the child he wants sae badly. Yet I could never love him as a wife should." She thought for a moment, gave Kenneth a squeeze, and continued, "I remember lying down that awful night with the wee cratur. I couldna sleep but listened to his breathing and watched him, so quiet and snug. I thought of Sam and Mary lying dead and how unconcerned for them that little fellow was, so helpless and trusting. And I thought of the terrible thing I had done to the Beast of Garth and found no remorse in me." She sighed, looked up at her husband and smiled.

"Aye Ken, I have not yet given ye the child you try so hard to put in me but we are lucky to have John." Kenneth laid his hand on her head and gently rubbed her scalp through her thick black hair. To see her smile was for him like seeing the blue sky through cold morning haar.

I felt like hugging and kissing them both but instead said something that was quite irrelevant.

"Och, it's not for you or Morag I feel sorry now. It is Beatrix Sinclair!" The two lovers looked at me and I blabbered on, "I knew that Alastair and she were going strong and before he left Megginch for home I teased him about wearing himself out on the Sinclair woman. I only wish," I stopped. My chatter had caught their attention. "I only wish I had been at Plewlands to see my mother's face when Beatrix marched up to the front door and presented her, first with Alastair's child and then with her marriage lines!"

The miracle happened. Morag and Kenneth burst out laughing.

"Aye," said Kenneth, "At least Morag and I dinna spit at each other like cats as those two can do. Mind you, it was a long time before this lass of mine accepted my clumsy efforts to comfort her. I think she had got it into her heid, Lady Jean, she might murder any other man wha lay with her!"

I winked at Morag, turned on Kenneth and laughed in his face. "You poor man," I said. "You must have risked your life a thousand times!"

Twenty-Seven

L ife at Plewlands makes me glad to be a Hogeston and to be married to such a man as Graham Hay. We have fought like mad things and I would not trust him out of my sight for long, yet I love his laughter, his great hugs, his shining eyes and I can forgive him almost anything. The more I see of my contemporaries the luckier I know myself to be. Some of my friends live so uncomfortably in the bonds of marriage. Even my sister Catherine although paired into a noble family has found wedlock more of a prison than the enchanted garden she had dreamed about. John Stewart has the reputation of a rake. So it is that at every mass I light a candle to the Virgin Mary.

The Madonna must have smiled on me the first time I made love with Graham. I was daft on him and I still am, but I shudder to imagine what could have happened had he not been as daft on me. During the summer of my sixteenth year, I was at Kildrummy with my cousins. Graham Hay was there too. I had seen him before, my strong beautiful boastful Graham, although I doubt he had ever noticed me. But now I was a woman, or about to become one. He had his eye on me, I knew, and it only required a little heart-twisting faith to believe that he would follow me when I rode down the hill from the castle to catch butterflies in the Howe of Alford. I was full of the most romantic ideas. When mothers talk to their daughters about such things, Bridget had let me into the secret of how she had conceived my eldest brother, among the woods and the birdsong of the Don at Kildrummy. The art in her story was to impress on me that such joys can only be reached through marriage. It misfired a bit. All I could think of, with Graham panting behind me, was the delicious naughtiness and the excitement of what I was going to do. I had a plan. I would take off my clothes, swim naked in the river and, like a water nymph, be caught there by my beloved as he came riding by. The act was very nearly spoiled. Graham was not so hard on my heels as I had thought and the river Don even in August runs deep and cold. It took a roaring fire to stop my teeth from chattering and a hard rub down with his saddle cloth before I was in any way in a fit state for his lovemaking.

I told Bridget about my "first time." She pretended to be very shocked. So I gave her the story of Kenneth and Morag and the Beast of Garth. We were in the small turret room in Plewlands. My mother reclined comfortably on a couch, her bare feet tucked under her hips. Beatrix lay in front of the fire, with her head supported by a hand, on one of father's outlandish rugs. It was the end of the day and the children were in bed. The two babes were in the room with us for they were both cutting teeth and fretful. I made a good story of it. When I had told them what I had seen at the croft of Dierdre I unwound the snake-jewel and held it up for them to see. The firelight shone in the green eyes of the two wildcats. Bridget rose and took the heavy gold chain from me and fastened it round her waist. Slowly she raised her long slim arms from her side and began to dance, moving her feet gently to music only she could hear then faster until her skirt billowed from her hips. She stopped and stood looking down at the heads of the wildcats where they lay high between her thighs.

"Another woman danced, much better than I can, before your father," she said. "She wore this golden chain. He swore to me that all she did was dance, but I do not believe that was all they did."

"Mariota Athyn, mistress of the Wolf of Badenoch," I breathed. "You think there was love between her and father?"

"Should I expect him to have been a saint as well as a priest?" She unclipped the gleaming jewel and let it trail from her fingers. "The stories that this piece of gold could tell!" she murmured.

"God be thanked it cannot."

Bridget tiptoed towards the two children. She bent and looked down on my Yolette.

"Little sweetheart," she said softly. "Yours is the name at the top of our family tree and from Yolette de Dreux you are descended both through my blood and through your grandfather Philip's. She was beautiful, that French princess, and married a King of Scotland in ancient times."

She turned and looked into the cradle where Beatrix's child lay sleeping.

"Philip Hogeston, my beloved," she whispered. "If your spirit hovers near this babe may this golden bauble appease it and exorcise The Curse of James." She hung the chain across the hood of the cradle, stooped and kissed her grandson's brow. "Grow strong, my pretty one. Grow clean and straight and free, my little Philip."

Bridget Hogeston stepped toward her daughter-in-law, knelt on the rug, took Beatrix's cheeks between her hands and kissed her. "Thank you Beatrix for taking into your body the seed of my son and all the Hogestons. Now my husband's soul can rest in peace."

Beatrix's face was a study. At that moment I think she wanted to embrace her mother-in-law. Instead, she returned her kiss but said quietly and with conviction.

"Aye, young Philip is a Hogeston. I have nae doots on thon score. But mind ye Bridget," she hesitated for she had never called my mother by her first name before, "Mind you, this loon o' mine is half a Sinclair and from what I hae heard, in wickedness, there is no sae muckle tae choose between them and the Hogestons of Plewlands."

Historical Notes

Queen Joan and the Black Knight of Lorn. Joan Beaufort, cousin of King Henry V of England, was wooed and wed by King James I of Scotland during the latter's captivity at the English court. In 1437 she was personally responsible for the torture and the horrific deaths meted out to the murderers of her husband. She bore the King seven children, including one son, who became King James II of Scotland. To protect the young King from the rival Regents, Livingston and Crichton, she married James Stewart, the Black Knight of Lorn, who sired three boys the youngest of which, Andrew, became a Bishop of Moray. The capture of the young King, his mother Queen Joan and her husband the Black Knight of Lorn by the Regent Livingston was a crucial episode in the unhappy strife-full years of the King's minority.

Donald Balloch, Lord of Isla. Closely related to MacDonald, Lord of the Isles, Donald Balloch commanded a great fleet of galleys with which he devastated the western seaboard of Scotland from Innerskip to Bute, the Cumbraes and Arran, returning to Isla with plunder said to number 500 horses, 10,000 cattle and pigs, 1,000 sheep and goats, 100 bolls of malt, and 100 merks of silver.

The Wolf of Badenoch. A son of King Robert II, Alexander Stewart married Euphemia, Countess of Ross, but lived with his mistress Mariota de Athyn in Lochindorb Castle. He was involved in prolonged litigation with Alexander Bur, Bishop of Moray, concerning land rights, a legal battle which ended in violence with the burnings of Forres and Elgin and the destruction of Elgin Cathedral in 1390.

Mariota de Athyn. This remarkable woman was bonded in love to her volatile husband and held him by her passion and by her beauty despite demands from Bishop Bur and from his brother King Robert III to cast her out and return to his lawful wife. She bore him six children, one of whom, Alexander, became an outstanding figure in Scottish history. Another, James, according to the narrative in a previous publication *The Wolf,* cursed Sir Philip Hogeston of Plewlands in Lochindorb Castle, a curse which came to roost at Dunstaffnage in the lands of Lorn.

James Stewart. The third son of the Wolf and Mariota, was co-partner in a child marriage with Janet Menzies at the age of twelve. Young Janet brought with her as part of her dowry, land in Appin of Dull, Strathtay, where the Wolf built Garth Castle. James and Janet occupied this fortress and had a son, John Gorm – John of the Blue Armour. James adopted the nickname "The fierce Wolf" but was better known to his many enemies, including the McIvor Clan of Glen Lyon, as Chuilein Churta – The Accursed Whelp.

John Gorm Stewart. When King James I of Scotland was slaughtered in Perth in 1437, John of the Blue Armour, Robert Reoch Chief of the Clan Robertson, and Black Colin of Rome, Laird of Glen Orchy, were prominent in the hunt for the King's murderers. John Gorm caught the ringleader Murdoch and was commended by the Estates (the Scottish Parliament). A talented swordsman, he died on the North Inch of Perth in 1443 fighting a band of brigands in defence of the Sheriff of Perth.

Bishop John Winchester. An Englishman, John de Winchester became the lifelong friend of King James I of Scotland. This friendship blossomed during the latter's detention at the English Court and took him to Scotland with the King and Queen in 1424 when James was reclaimed by his people for a very large sum of money. During the long minority of King James II, John Winchester travelled frequently to England as a Scottish emissary, his advice being valued by both governments probably because of his dual nationality and his legal astuteness. He was a Bachelor of Common Law, Provost of Lincluden and Lord Registrar of Scotland before being consecrated in 1437 as Bishop of Moray at the Monastery of Cambuskenneth. His long and capable life ended in 1466 and he lies buried under his sepulchre in St. Mary's Aisle of Elgin Cathedral.